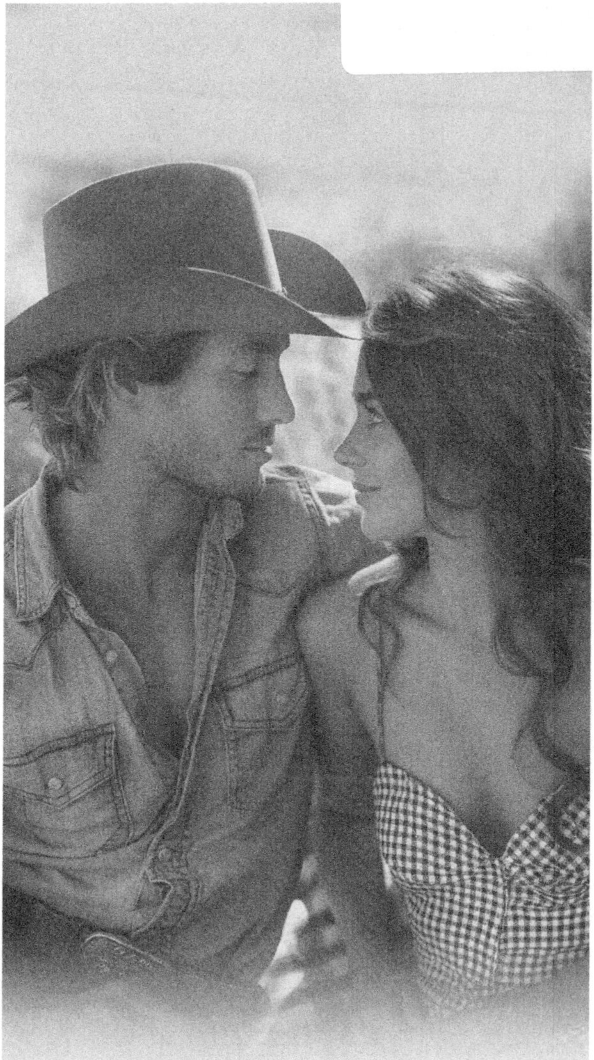

CW01217464

WRANGLING A HOT SUMMER COWBOY

Copyright © May 2024 by Katie Lane

All rights reserved. Except for use in any review, the reproduction or utilization of this work in whole or in part in any form by any electronic, mechanical or other means, now known or hereinafter invented, including xerography, photocopying and recording, or in any information storage or retrieval system, is forbidden without the written permission of the publisher.

This book is a work of fiction. Names, characters, places, and incidents are a product of the writer's imagination. All rights reserved. Scanning, uploading, and electronic sharing of this book without the permission of the author is unlawful piracy and theft. To obtain permission to excerpt portions of the text, please contact the author at *katie@katielanebooks.com*

Thank you for respecting this author's hard work and livelihood.

Cover Design and Interior Format
© KILLION
GROUP INC.

Wrangling a HOT SUMMER COWBOY

HOLIDAY RANCH FOUR

KATIE LANE

*To Gabriella James, my sweet summer girl.
Never stop shining your brilliant light, Gabs.*

Chapter One

IT WAS AN image straight out of a country dream.

Miles and miles of land stretched out for as far as the eye could see. Land filled with mesquite trees, scrub oak, late spring wildflowers, and early summer grasses. A herd of longhorn cattle lazily munched on those grasses, their tails occasionally lifting to flick at pesky insects. Or maybe just to fan their bodies in the sizzling May heat.

Amid the land and cattle sat a big red barn and quaint two-story farmhouse. The barn brought up images of six laughing girls grooming thoroughbred horses and cuddling newborn kittens and jumping in shrieks of delight from the hayloft. The farmhouse with its wide porch brought up another image.

An image of a loving family.

As always, the image caused Corbin Whitlock to feel numerous things: pain, desire, envy, and anger. The anger always won out. It was a much easier emotion to deal with than the others.

"I don't know how in the hell I let you and Jesse talk me into allowing the Holidays to stay for a month, Sunshine Brook Whitlock," he grumbled as he maneuvered his truck around a pothole in the road. "I should have my head examined."

His sister smiled at him from the passenger seat. Sunny had been aptly named. She was brilliance and warmth and life.

She was certainly his life.

"I'm not going to argue that point, Corbin Conrad Whitlock," she said. "I have never understood the things that go on in your head."

"Just like I don't understand the things that go on in yours. Allowing the Holidays to stay for a month will only make it harder for them to leave." He took his eyes off the dirt road to give her a stern look. "And they are going to leave, Sunny. They aren't like all the stray animals you kept bringing home when we were kids."

Not that they had ever been able to keep any of those strays. Which probably explained why Corbin had grown so attached to Taylor Swift. He glanced down at the tiger-striped kitten curled up in his lap and gently stroked her soft, tiny head as he continued.

"The Holidays aren't strays. They have six daughters who I'm sure will be more than happy to take them in. Or at least four of them will."

Sunny laughed. "Don't tell me you're still holding a grudge against Liberty and Belle for that little high school prank they pulled. I've pulled worse pranks than that."

Sunny did have a prankster nature, but her jokes were all in good fun. Liberty and Belle's prank hadn't been fun. Not fun at all. When he didn't say anything, Sunny sighed.

"Okay. I guess my pranks never broke anyone's heart."

"Liberty didn't break my heart. You have to be in love with someone for them to break your heart and I was never in love with her."

"No, just infatuated. And since you're taking their family's ranch, I have to wonder if you weren't infatuated with the entire Holiday family."

He snorted. "Not hardly. Like I've told you and Jesse repeatedly. Foreclosing on this ranch isn't about the Holidays." He glanced at her. "I want you to have your dream home."

She opened her mouth as if to say something, but then closed it again and smiled brightly. "Thank you, big brother. You always have given me everything I've dreamed of. Now about that Lamborghini for my birthday?"

He looked back at the road. "Not a chance. After the way you were driving in Paris, I'm not about to buy you a fast car." He pulled in behind the U-Haul truck he'd been following to the ranch. "I ordered you a Subaru. They're supposed to be some of the safest cars on the road."

Sunny rolled her eyes as she reached for the door handle. "Whoopee. I just love playing it safe."

Corbin didn't find her sarcasm funny. Keeping Sunny safe was a full-time job. While he had always been cautious, she had always been adventurous and a daredevil. She never did anything illegal—besides driving way too fast—but she was always willing to try something new, exciting . . . and dangerous.

Against his wishes, she'd skydived, mountain climbed, and scuba dived with sharks. She'd driven Formula One race cars and motocross motorcycles and taken flying lessons. After graduating from college, she'd wanted to travel all over the world. He'd put his foot down and closed his wallet on that dream. But she had talked him into going to an art school in Paris.

Corbin had been worried sick the entire three years she'd been gone—even with the security team he'd hired to keep an eye on her.

But she was home now. Their home. And he could finally relax.

Although, as he climbed out of his truck, he didn't feel relaxed. A knot of unease, anxiety . . . and guilt settled in his stomach. It pissed him off. He had every right to be there. The Holidays had known what would happen if they failed to make the loan payments on the ranch. He wasn't at fault. He had only done what any smart businessman would do.

The Holidays would find another place to call home. In fact, at their age, they should probably be living in a retirement community. A ranch this size was too much for three old people to handle by themselves. The debt they had gotten themselves in proved it.

But knowing that didn't stop his guilt from growing when Mitzy Holiday, or Mimi as everyone called her, came around the side of the house.

The Holidays' grandma looked like she had every other time he'd visited the ranch—like she'd been rolling around in the dirt. Her gardening gloves, T-shirt, jeans, and roper boots were covered in dark soil. There was even a smudge on her nose and the wide brim of her hat.

Completely unconcerned with the dirt, Sunny hurried over and gave her a tight hug. Sunny had fallen in love with Mimi after only one meeting. Which wasn't surprising given that Sunny seemed to love everyone . . . while Corbin only tolerated people.

And Sunny wasn't the only female in Corbin's life that had fallen in love with Mimi. Tay woke up from her slumber and took one look at the old woman and started struggling to be let down. But since there were way too many dangers on a ranch for a tiny kitten, Corbin kept a tight hold as Mimi walked over to greet Tay with an ear scratch.

"Hello, sweet girl." Mimi looked at Corbin. "It's a good thing you're moving in early. My arthritis tells me it's going to rain this afternoon. Which is why everyone is busy getting the ranch work done early."

Corbin didn't have a clue what ranch work she was talking about. His sister's pleas weren't the only reason he'd let the Holidays stay for a month. There were a lot of things Corbin didn't know about running a ranch. Something his sister was well aware of. If her twinkling eyes were any indication, Sunny was thoroughly enjoying his discomfort.

"Then I guess we need to get these boxes unpacked so Corbin can help with that ranch work," she said with a smug smile. "After all, this is your ranch now, Cory."

He shot her an annoyed look before he headed over to the movers and started issuing orders about where he wanted them to put the boxes.

There weren't that many. He had to wonder why he'd even bothered to hire men to help them move. After moving so much when they were kids, he and Sunny had learned to travel light. Or possibly live light. Sunny had brought very little back with her from Europe. Since Corbin planned to keep the penthouse in Houston for when he traveled there on business, he had left all the furniture and household items. He would worry about buying more for the ranch once the Holidays had moved out. For now, he'd only brought clothes, books, personal items, and his office equipment. Not wanting the moving men to drop the box with his laptop and printer, he handed Tay to Sunny and grabbed it.

Darla Holiday was there to greet them when they stepped in the door.

"Corbin! Sunny! We're so happy you're here." She had always been nice and welcoming, but he struggled to reciprocate. With her dark hair and soft green eyes, she looked like Liberty and Belle. She glanced at the box he carried. "I bet you'll want that in the study."

He expected the study to be filled with ranch business files, family photographs, and Hank's personal items, but it had been completely cleaned out.

As was the upstairs bedroom she showed him to next.

"We figured you'd want the room with the biggest bed." Darla plumped one of the pillows. "This was Liberty and Belle's room. We got them twin beds like the other girls, but they flat refused to sleep separately so we had to get them a queen. Which is ironic since they're twins."

Corbin didn't laugh. He wasn't happy about sleeping in the twins' room. Not happy at all. But he couldn't say anything. Not when Sunny was standing there and he'd just gotten through telling her he wasn't still holding a grudge. So he kept his silence as Darla directed Sunny to the room next door. When they were gone, he released a grumbled cuss and stroked Tay's head as he glanced around.

At least there were no pictures or high school mementos. Nothing to remind him of a time he'd just as soon forget.

Although there was a scent. A citrusy scent that wiggled its way into his nose and brought with it memories of emerald eyes and raven hair and a husky laugh that would make any young boy become infatuated.

But Corbin wasn't a young boy anymore. Lemony scents and a soft, husky laugh no longer made him feel lightheaded and dopey. As an attractive man who ran a successful business, he'd had his fair share of relationships. He'd discovered most women were interested in two things: his bank account and a wedding ring. He never divulged his net worth and he never wanted to get married. Witnessing his parents' bond in unholy matrimony had been more than enough for him.

That wasn't the case with Sunny. She didn't remember their parents' knock-down-drag-out fights and had forgiven them long ago for dumping their two kids on every relative willing to take them.

Corbin struggled with forgiveness.

And forgetting.

The movers arrived with his boxes and Tay's things. He had them place the cat condo next to the window so she could look out and her box of toys in the closet, but when they brought in the high-tech litter box he'd just bought, he shook his head.

"Take that down to the laundry room." He picked up Tay. "I'll show you where it is."

Once it was set up in a corner of the laundry room, he placed Tay inside the domed compartment so she could do her business. The kitten peeked out the opening of the space-age-looking dome as if to say WTF.

He laughed. "I know it's weird looking, but—"

"That's putting it mildly. What in tarnation is that contraption?"

He glanced up to find Mimi standing in the doorway. Her gardening hat was missing and her fine white hair looked like a bedraggled feather duster.

"It's a self-cleaning litter box."

"Well, isn't that fancy." She stepped in to get a closer look. "Where does the cat poop go?"

"There's a drum that spins and sifts it out and it falls into the airtight tray at the bottom."

She shook her head. "The things folks think of." Tay jumped out of the litter box and greeted Mimi with loud meows. She picked up the cat and cuddled her close. The fact Tay didn't scratch or nip her proved how much she loved the old woman. The kitten had never been much of a cuddler—except with Corbin. And it had taken him weeks to earn the cat's trust.

"So you all moved in?" Mimi asked.

"Not yet. I figured I'd set up my office first. I have some emails I need to send."

She hesitated. "You do realize we don't have Wi-Fi, right?"

He stared at her in disbelief. Who didn't have Wi-Fi in this day and age?

Obviously, the Holidays.

"Liberty tried to get someone to come out and fix it," Mimi continued. "But getting fix-it folks to drive all the way out here isn't easy." She smiled. "But I think it was a blessing in disguise. If we'd had Wi-Fi, all Liberty would have done was work and she never would have fallen in love with your brother."

Corbin tried not to scowl. He wasn't at all thrilled about Liberty and Jesse falling in love. And it had nothing to do with any leftover feelings Corbin had for Liberty. He was worried about Jesse getting hurt. But his half brother was smart. He was the one who had helped Corbin make most of his money. Corbin figured Jesse would see Liberty's true colors eventually.

"Maybe taking a break from work will be a blessing for you too." Mimi said. "Now that you own a ranch, you might as well enjoy it. Sunny already headed out to look around her new home."

The thought of Sunny getting lost on the big ranch—or worse, hurt—had him immediately concerned.

"Where did she go?"

"She was headed to the barn last time I saw her. But there's no need to worry. We don't have any aggressive animals that will harm her. Just a horse, and I'm sure your sister is smart enough to not go riding in a thunderstorm."

Corbin panicked. That was exactly something his sister would do.

"I need to go check on her." He started to take Tay, but Mimi stopped him.

"Why don't you leave her? I promise to keep her safe."

Corbin might not trust the other Holidays as far as he could throw them, but as he looked into Mimi's direct eyes, he realized he trusted her. He nodded before he headed out the back door.

As soon as he stepped outside, his concern for his sister grew. Mimi was right. The clear blue skies of the morning had been covered with a layer of angry dark clouds that rumbled with thunder. Halfway to the barn the sky opened up and a deluge of water rained down. By the time he got inside, he was drenched from head to toe.

He took off his hat and shook the water from it as he glanced around.

He had been inside the big red barn on more than one occasion. His uncle had been the foreman for the Holiday Ranch when Corbin and Sunny had first come to live with him and he had brought them out to the ranch numerous times before Hank Holiday fired him for drinking on the job.

"Sunny!" he called.

The only answer was the rain hitting the roof and the flutter of wings. He glanced up to the rafters. A few doves perched there, their beady eyes staring down at him as if questioning his right to be there.

He unsnapped his soaked western shirt and stripped it off as he moved farther into the barn. It smelled like fresh hay and manure. No doubt from the horse that poked his head out of one of the stalls. Corbin sighed in relief. At least he didn't have to worry about Sunny being tossed off a runaway horse and breaking her neck.

He hung his hat and shirt on the stall door across from the horse. "Hey, there, big guy."

The horse eyeballed him before he tossed his head and showed his teeth.

Damn, those were big teeth.

As a kid, he'd dreamed of owning a horse and becoming a cowboy. His Aunt May had loved Clint Eastwood as much as she'd loved the oxycodone her doctor had prescribed for her bad back. For the year and a half he and Sunny had lived with her, he had become infatuated with

Clint's spaghetti westerns and learning to ride a horse . . . while wearing a really cool poncho. When they came to Wilder, Corbin had hoped his dream would come true. But Uncle Dan had been fired before he could teach Corbin how to ride. Not that Uncle Dan would have ever gotten around to teaching him. Kids hadn't been his thing. He'd only agreed to let them live with him because he owed their daddy money.

Now, Corbin was a little leery of horses. He'd had a bad experience horseback riding and hadn't attempted to ride again. But if he was going to become a rancher, he needed to get over his fear.

He reached out to pet the horse when a loud whinny had him snatching his hand back. Except the whinny hadn't come from the horse in front of him. He turned toward the open doors just in time to see a wild-eyed horse come charging through the sheet of rain.

Corbin's heart almost jumped out of his chest.

Not only because of the charging beast . . . but also because of the stunning woman who rode it.

Chapter Two

BELLE JUSTINE HOLIDAY had always made bad decisions. At the grocery store, she always chose the slowest line. At a restaurant, she always chose the menu item that had the waiter wincing. At the gym, she always chose the treadmill that sped up erratically. She chose clothing that looked great in the dressing room but hideous when she got it home, makeup that made her skin look yellow and sallow, and haircuts that were thirty years out of style.

If left to her own devices, she would look like a homeless person stuck in the nineties and inflicted with jaundice.

Thankfully, she had never been left to her own devices.

She had her twin sister. Liberty had never made a bad decision in her life. Every choice she made was the right one. Grocery lines, menu items, treadmills, clothes, makeup, and hairstyles. Flowers, food catering, and wedding venues. If Liberty chose it, it always turned out perfectly.

And Liberty loved choosing things—not only for herself, but also for her twin.

Unfortunately, when Liberty wasn't around, things went to hell in a handcart.

The current situation was a perfect example.

If Liberty had been around this morning when Belle had decided to ride over to their family's ranch, she wouldn't have allowed Belle to choose a horse that happened to be terrified of thunder. In fact, she would have taken one look at the clouds gathering in the sky and decided it would be better to drive to the Holiday Ranch.

But Liberty hadn't been there. She had been with Jesse. Jesse Cates, a man Belle was thoroughly starting to dislike for taking her sister away from her and leaving Belle to her own bad decision-making.

And he wasn't just taking Liberty away from her. He was also taking Liberty away from her and Belle's business.

Holiday Sisters Events was Belle's life. She loved helping people celebrate the most important events in their lives. She loved fluffing wedding veils, lighting ninety birthday candles, and helping fifty-year-wedding-anniversary couples remember the vows they wrote. She loved making sure the arrangements on the reception tables were correctly placed, the cake wasn't cut until it was time, and the flower girls didn't toss all the petals before they walked down the aisle.

What she didn't love was all the decisions that went along with the perfect event. Decisions were Liberty's forte. Without her, there would be no Holiday Sisters Events.

Thunder boomed and the horse whinnied and

reared. Belle was so busy trying to keep her seat she didn't notice there was someone in the barn until they spoke.

"What the hell!"

As soon as the horse's front hoofs landed on the ground, Belle glanced around until she spied the shirtless man standing by the back stalls. It didn't take more than a second to figure out who he was. Corbin Whitlock was the reason Belle was there. Although he barely resembled the sweet, awkward boy she'd known in high school.

His hair, that had once been a mop of unruly dark blond curls, was now trimmed short on the sides. Even wet, the locks on top fell in expertly cut layers. His face was no longer dotted with acne. It was blemish free, tanned, and clean shaven. The tall, gangly body, which had tripped over its large feet whenever Liberty was around, was not gangly anymore. It was sculpted with hard chest muscles, knotted biceps, and washboard abs.

The only features remotely familiar were the blue eyes that stared back at her. But even those had changed. They no longer held the soft vulnerability that had touched Belle's heart.

Now, they were hard and cold.

"Bella."

While everyone else called her Belle or Belly, Corbin had always called her Bella. She never knew why, but being a big Twilight fan, she had liked it.

She didn't like it so much now. Especially when his voice held no warmth. Although she wasn't surprised by his cool tone. She knew he hated her and why. But she was surprised that he had recognized her. Few people outside her family could tell the difference between her and Liberty. How had Corbin known the difference? Especially when she was soaking wet and they hadn't seen each other since high school.

Lady Grantham snorted and restlessly pranced and Corbin took a step back and warily eyeballed the horse. Which surprised her. He had been an awkward teenager, but never a fearful one. His courting of the most popular girl in school had proved it.

"What the hell are you doing?" His voice was deeper than she remembered. Huskier. Angrier.

"I think that should be obvious—coming in out of the rain."

"Well, you can go right back out in it. I have enough Holidays to deal with. You aren't welcome here."

Not welcome here? On a ranch that had belonged to her family for over a hundred years? She knew she had done Corbin wrong. But the stupid, teenage mistake she had made years ago wasn't justification for thinking he could steal her family's ranch. But before she could do something really stupid—like lose her temper and tell him off—another loud boom of thunder caused Lady Grantham to rear again.

This time, Belle was too preoccupied to be prepared. She slipped out of the wet saddle and hit the hard-packed ground on her butt with a pain-filled grunt. It wasn't the first time she had been thrown from a horse. She was country smart enough to roll out of the way as the frightened horse charged back out into the rain.

She was lying there trying to catch her breath and assess her injuries when a warm hand settled on the chilled skin of her arm and gently rolled her over.

"Bella." This time, Corbin didn't say her name like a curse as he knelt next to her. The one word was spoken in a soft, concerned voice. She had forgotten how blue his eyes were. They were like the sky at dusk, deep, intense cobalt that could rival any flamboyant display the setting sun offered.

"It's okay. Everything is going to be okay." He pulled a cellphone from the back pocket of his wet jeans and tapped the screen. "Just stay still. An ambulance will be here shortly."

She closed her fingers around his wrist. The man had one thick wrist. And an extremely strong heartbeat. His pulse thumped wildly against her fingertips as she spoke unsteadily.

"I-I-I'm—fine."

"Like hell you are. You just got thrown off a wild-eyed beast from hell and then trampled beneath his hoofs." He started tapping the screen again, but stopped when a snort of laughter bubbled out of her mouth.

"A wild-eyed beast from hell?"

He lowered the phone. "You think this is funny? Did you get kicked in the head?"

She stopped laughing, but still couldn't keep the smile from her face. "You're right. It's not a laughing matter. But Lady Grantham isn't a wild-eyed beast from hell. She was just scared."

"So you aren't hurt?" His gaze swept over her before it settled on her chest. She glanced down and realized the rain had turned her white T-shirt transparent.

Another bad choice.

She crossed her arms over her chest. Which caused his gaze to quickly lift to her eyes. Was he blushing? Or just flushed from the muggy heat of the barn?

"The only thing that's hurt is my pride," she said. "Although that's not the first time I've been thrown from a horse and I doubt it will be the last."

"You've been thrown before and you still ride? That's insane."

"Some people might think so, but to me, the occasional fall is worth the joy of riding."

"I don't think any joy is worth the fall you took. Can you sit up?" He slid his hands behind her shoulders and gently lifted her, bringing her face only inches from his hard chest. He smelled of rain and manly soap. Her lungs absorbed the scent like a dry sponge to water and she felt a little lightheaded.

Had she gotten kicked in the head? This was the man who had foreclosed on her family's ranch. She shouldn't be sniffing him like a dog in heat and getting lightheaded. She was there for one reason and one reason only and that was to apologize for the bad choice she'd made years before.

"You okay?" he asked.

She pulled her gaze away from the sexy hollow between his hard pectoral muscles and nodded. "I'm good." His gaze lowered to her breasts again and he cleared his throat and looked away.

"So do you want to explain what you were doing horseback riding in a thunderstorm?"

"It wasn't raining when I left the Remington Ranch."

He looked back at her. "So you're staying with your sister Cloe?"

Cloe had recently married the oldest Remington boy, something Belle still found hard to believe. Not only because her older sister had never expressed any interest in Rome, but also because Rome's daddy had long been Hank Holiday's sworn enemy. Subsequently, their children had never been close. Which made her stay at the Remington Ranch more than a little uncomfortable.

Not just that, but Cloe and Rome were still newlyweds. Belle shouldn't be staying with them. She should be staying at the Holiday Ranch . . . with Liberty. But Liberty was living with Jesse at the house he recently purchased to turn into a bed-and-breakfast.

It wasn't right.

Nothing was right.

Belle had to fix this topsy-turvy world before she ended up toppling off into nothingness.

Which was why she was there. She was the only one who knew exactly what had happened in high school. The only one to blame for Corbin's hatred of the Holidays. As much as she would have liked to forget that night had ever happened, she couldn't if she wanted to save her family's ranch. After she fixed things here, she needed to convince Liberty that living in a rundown mansion with Jesse was a crazy idea. Then maybe everything could go back to normal.

She just wanted things to go back to normal.

She took a deep breath before she spoke. "I came here today to apologize for what happened that night."

"I don't know what night you're referring to." The coldness that entered his eyes said differently.

She swallowed hard. "The night you were supposed to go on a date with Liberty."

Something flashed in his eyes. Anger? Hurt? Before she could figure it out, he looked away. "Water under the bridge." He got to his feet. "I'll tell your family that you're here."

She tried to get up, but her abused butt protested the quick movement and she groaned in pain.

He whirled back around. "You are hurt."

Her butt was only bruised, but she knew if she told him that, he'd leave. She couldn't let him leave until she'd convinced him to let her family keep their home.

"Maybe a little." She winced as she slowly got to her feet, then limped toward a bale of hay. She only made it halfway before she was lifted off her feet and held against a hard, naked chest. Being surrounded by Corbin's hot skin felt like diving beneath a heated blanket. She couldn't help feeling disappointed when he lowered her to the hay bale and stepped away.

"I'm calling an ambulance." He lifted his phone.

"No! Really. I'm fine. I just need a minute to—" She hesitated. "Tell you how sorry I am. I shouldn't have pretended to be Liberty. I should have told you immediately who I was and explained things. I take full responsibility."

He laughed, but there was no humor in it. "You take full responsibility? I think I know who is responsible. Everyone in Wilder knows Liberty is the leader and you're just her minion."

It was the truth, but that didn't stop his words from stinging.

"I'm not her minion."

He cocked an eyebrow. "Really? Tell me one thing you haven't done that she's wanted you to do?" She scrambled for an answer and came up with nothing. He snorted. "Like I thought. So don't try to tell me you were responsible for the twin switch. You might have tried to execute it, but it wasn't your idea."

"It was my idea. I was only supposed to tell you that Liberty was sick. But when I came to the door and you looked . . ." She hesitated and he finished the sentence for her.

"Like an infatuated fool."

"I was going to say like you had spent a lot of time getting ready."

Anger hardened his face. "So you felt sorry for me."

"No!" When his eyebrows lifted, she sighed. "Fine. I felt badly that you were going to be disappointed and when you mistook me for Liberty and handed me the flowers, I just thought . . . what would it hurt if I pretended to be her for just one night? I didn't think you would figure it out."

"Only an idiot wouldn't. You're nothing like Liberty."

Since Liberty was gregarious, charming, and dynamic, he was pretty much saying Belle had been reserved, boring, and dull. And yet, he had continued to play along.

"Why didn't you say something?" she asked.

He shrugged. "I guess I wanted to see how far you'd go."

She had gone far. Too far. But that wasn't something she was willing to talk about. And he didn't seem to want to talk about it either. Although his gaze lowered to her mouth for a split second before he looked away.

"I'm not going to give your family's ranch back. So if that's what this confession is all about, you've wasted your time. Foreclosing on the ranch was never about the prank you pulled that night. It was about your family defaulting on their loan."

She stood, trying not to wince when pain shot through her butt. "My brother-in-law, Rome, is willing to pay you what we owe."

He shrugged. "I don't want money. I want the ranch."

"Then buy someone else's. There are plenty of ranches for sale around here. This isn't your home."

In the depths of his blue eyes was the vulnerability that had been missing before—the same vulnerability that had pierced Belle's heart on the night he had come to pick up Liberty and Liberty had already left on another date. Like then, Belle wanted to remove that look and replace it with something else. Happiness. Laughter. Hope. But then the look was gone and when he spoke, his voice held no warmth or forgiveness.

Just determination.

"It is now."

Chapter Three

Corbin had vowed hell would freeze over before he touched a Holiday sister again.

Well, hell had frozen over.

And it didn't look like it was going to thaw out anytime soon.

As much as he would love to order Belle off his ranch, he couldn't do it. Not when she was injured and it was raining cats and dogs. But he wasn't about to be nice either.

"Can you walk?"

"Yes, I can walk." The words were snappish. She was pissed. Had she really thought he'd hand over her family's ranch just because she had apologized? It only confirmed the Holidays' arrogance.

"Good. Because I'm sure as hell not carrying you into the house." He turned and headed for the door, grabbing his shirt and hat on the way and pulling them on. He didn't know if she followed and he didn't care. Okay, maybe he did care. Once they were out in the storm, he couldn't help glancing over his shoulder.

Her head was lowered against the driving rain

and she limped as if every step caused her pain. With a muttered curse, he turned around and lifted her up in his arms, bending his head so his cowboy hat shielded her face from the majority of rain.

"I said I can walk," she grumbled.

He trudged toward the porch, ignoring her. What he couldn't ignore was the way she felt in his arms. For a tall woman, she weighed practically nothing. One arm curved around his shoulders while the other was folded in front of her, her hand clutching his shirt as if he planned to drop her. Her lemony scent filled his lungs every time he took a breath.

When they got to the porch, Mimi was holding open the door. "I was just coming to look for you. Belle?"

Belle lifted a hand and smiled weakly. "Hey, Mimi."

Mimi didn't look at all upset to see her granddaughter in Corbin's arms. In fact, a smile spread over her face as she motioned them in. "Come on in here, you two. You're soaked to the skin." Once inside, he started to put Belle down, but Mimi stopped him. "Take her to the laundry room, Cory, and I'll bring y'all some towels."

Sunny was the only one he let get away with calling him Cory. Which reminded him of why he'd gone out to the barn in the first place. The thought of his sister being out in the storm caused a stab of fear to slice through him.

"Did Sunny come back?"

Mimi nodded. "She got caught in the storm,

but she's fine. Hank found her and she's changing into some dry clothes as we speak. Which is what y'all need to do."

Relieved, Corbin followed Mimi's orders and carried Belle to the laundry room. Darla was cooking something at the stove in the kitchen. She stopped when she saw them and hurried after them.

"Corbin? Belle? What happened? Don't tell me you two were out in this nasty storm. And why is Corbin carrying you, Belle? Are you hurt?"

"It's nothing, Mama." Belle sent him a pleading look. "Corbin is just a gentleman and didn't want me walking through puddles."

He sat her down on the bench by the door. "She was thrown off a horse and might need to see a doctor."

Darla gasped and hurried over. "Oh, sweet Lord, Belle. What were you doing on a horse in the middle of a thunderstorm?"

Belle shot him an exasperated glare before she answered her mother. "It wasn't raining when I started out from the Remington Ranch. And I'm fine. I don't need to see a doctor. But I do need to call Cloe and make sure Lady Grantham gets home."

"I'll call Cloe once I make sure you're okay. Lift your arms and legs and wiggle your hands and feet."

Belle rolled her eyes. "I'm not a kid who needs to do the hokey pokey before you know I'm okay. I'm an adult woman who knows if some thing is broken. Besides a bruised behind, I'm fine, Mama."

Since Belle's physical health wasn't any of his business, Corbin should have kept his mouth shut. He didn't. "Then why were you limping?"

She glanced at him. "If you ever take a spill from a horse, you'll understand."

"A sore butt does make walking and sitting difficult." Mimi came into the room carrying towels. She handed one to Corbin and then one to Belle. "It's not the first time Belle has fallen off a horse, Darla. I'm sure she's fine. Although she needs to get out of those wet clothes and into a hot shower." She glanced at Corbin's open shirt and her eyebrows lifted. "It looks like you already started getting out of yours."

Before Corbin could do more than self-consciously hold his shirt closed, she clapped her hands. "Well, don't just stand there dripping water on the floor, Cory. Get those boots off, towel off, and get upstairs."

Again, Corbin found himself following her orders. While he hung his hat, toed off his boots, and dried his hair, Darla and Mimi carefully removed Belle's boots and fussed over her. He couldn't help feeling a little resentful. Not for himself, but for his sister. Sunny had never had a mother figure fuss over her.

Which probably explained why Corbin did.

When he was as dry as he could get with his wet shirt and jeans still on, Corbin tossed the towel in the washing machine and headed out of the room. Whatever Darla was cooking smelled delicious. Since he hadn't eaten lunch and was starving, he couldn't help stopping to peek into the pot on the stove. The chicken and dumplings bubbling away in thick gravy made his mouth water. So did the cherry pie sitting on the counter cooling.

He glanced behind him to make sure no one was watching before he quickly snapped off a piece of crust and popped it into his mouth. It melted against his tongue like flaky butter and he snapped off another piece before he headed for the stairs.

There had to be over twelve steps that led to the second floor. All he could think about was how difficult it would be climbing them with a bruised butt. When Belle came limping around the corner, he muttered a cussword before he lifted her into his arms and carried her up the stairs.

"Would you stop it? I can walk."

"Not well."

"What's going on?" Sunny stood at the top of the stairs. Her hair was wet and Tay was cradled in one arm. The sight made him smile. It had taken a while for Tay to get used to his sister. He was glad they were getting along. Although the kitten started meowing and wiggling to get down when she saw Corbin.

"Belle got tossed off a horse." He put Belle down and took Tay from his sister.

Sunny looked at Belle with stunned surprise. "And my brother came to your rescue?" She glanced at him. "One of the meanie high school girls?"

Corbin had never slugged his sister and he never would, but there were times, like this one, when he wanted to.

He scowled and she laughed. "Sorry, big brother, but I'm just a little surprised. I thought you would hate the Holiday twins forever."

"He didn't have a choice," Belle said. "He was the only one there when it happened."

"Ahh." Sunny nodded. "Then that explains it. No matter how big of a meanie you are, my brother can't ignore a damsel in distress." She looked at Tay cuddled in his arm. "That cat is the perfect example. Tay scratched the hell out of him when he first got her and still he couldn't toss her out in the cold."

"She didn't scratch the hell out of me."

"That's not what Jesse told me."

"You and Jesse talk too much."

"And you don't talk enough." She hooked an arm through Belle's and pulled her down the hall. "Speaking of talking, I need all the details. How did you get tossed off a horse and what was my brother doing there when he's terrified of horses?"

Corbin watched them walk away and knew he was in trouble. Sunny had never had a filter. Which meant Belle would get to hear more about his life than he wanted her to. But there was nothing he could do about it. He had never been able to stop Sunny from being Sunny.

He headed for the bathroom.

He ran out of hot water halfway through his shower. He figured that had to do with Belle taking one at the same time. An image of a naked, soap-slick body popped into his head, but he pushed it right back out.

After he stepped out of the shower, he realized he had forgotten to bring clean clothes with him. He wrapped a towel around his waist and then peeked out the door to make sure no one was in the hall before he hurried to his room. He slipped inside without running into anyone and then almost jumped out of his skin when he turned and saw Jesse reclining on the bed with a pudgy pug snoring softly on his chest.

"Geez, Jess! You scared the shit out of me."

Jesse scowled. "You know what scares the shit out of me? Your cat. She attacked poor Buck Owens like a disgruntled tiger when all he wanted to do was say hi."

Corbin's muscles tightened. "If that dog of yours hurt Tay—"

"Relax. I wouldn't let Buck hurt her. Not that he would. Unlike your pet, he's a sweetheart." He tousled the pug's ears and the dog woke up and licked his face as he laughed.

"Tay is a sweetheart when she wants to be." Corbin glanced around. "Where is she?"

"She's with Mimi. For some reason, that woman has the magic touch." Jesse sat up and Buck jumped to the floor and started sniffing around. "So how did moving day go?"

"Not well," he grumbled as he closed the door

and walked to the dresser. "There's no Wi-Fi and Belle showed up in the middle of a rainstorm and got tossed off the horse she was riding."

"So I heard. Liberty completely lost it until she discovered her sister was okay." He paused. "I'm glad you were there to help her. All I can say is I'm proud of you, Whitty. I know it wasn't easy for you since you're still not over what happened in high school."

"I'm over it!" he snapped as the door opened and Liberty walked in. He had pulled on his boxer briefs, but that was all. He couldn't help holding the T-shirt he'd just taken out of the drawer in front of him like some blushing virgin.

Liberty didn't look at all embarrassed to walk in on a man dressing. "Oops. I didn't realize you had taken my room."

"I didn't take anything," he said. "This is the room your mother gave me."

She held up her hands. "Don't get your panties in a bunch." She glanced down and smirked. "Or should I say boxers."

Jesse laughed. "Stop teasing, Libby Lou. Can't you see you're embarrassing Whitty?"

"Sorry, Whitty." She didn't leave. Instead, she crouched down to greet Buck who was wiggling around with excitement. "Hey, my sweet boy."

"What am I?" Jesse said. "Chopped liver?"

She moved over to the bed and looped her arms around his neck. "You are my sweet man." She kissed him. And not a short kiss.

Corbin rolled his eyes. "Do you mind? I'm trying to get dressed. And what are you two doing here at the ranch? I don't remember inviting you."

Jesse and Liberty broke apart and Jesse grinned. "We sorta invited ourselves." He exchanged glances with Liberty. "We have a big surprise we're going to announce at dinner."

Corbin hated surprises as much as he hated being surrounded by Holidays.

But not more than thirty minutes later, that's where he found himself, sitting at the big harvest table in the kitchen, surrounded.

Besides Hank, Darla, Mimi, and the twins, there was the oldest sister, Sweetie Mae, who had been just as popular in high school as Liberty and was now a songwriter for a Nashville recording company. She was there with her husband, Decker Carson, who was the town sheriff. The second oldest Holiday sister, Cloe, was there with her husband, Rome Remington, whose family owned one of the biggest ranches in Texas. The two younger sisters, Hallie and Noelle, were the only Holidays missing. According to Darla, the storm had kept them from traveling from Austin and Dallas to share in Liberty and Jesse's surprise.

They hadn't missed anything. The surprise was ridiculous.

Jesse had bought a whorehouse that had been as famous as the Chicken Ranch. Corbin could understand Jesse being intrigued by the house and its sordid history, but he could not understand him wanting to turn the old mansion into a bed-and-breakfast. Jesse didn't make bad business choices. His bank account proved it. So did all the knowledge he'd imparted to Corbin. Without Jesse's help—and his money—Corbin's company, Oleander Investments, wouldn't be nearly as successful.

As he listened to Liberty go on and on about the bed-and-breakfast, he realized Jesse wasn't the one who had come up with the idea. Liberty had. It looked like she was controlling Jesse like she controlled her sister.

Jesse didn't seem to mind.

Nor did he seem to mind being surrounded by Holidays. He complimented Darla's chicken and dumplings and teased Mimi about being the prettiest gardener in Texas. He joked around with Hank and volunteered to help him and Rome brand some new calves.

But mostly Jesse watched Liberty with a besotted look on his face.

"I can't wait for y'all to see the plans," Liberty gushed. "Each room is going to be decorated for a Holiday sister. Hallie's will be decorated in black and white with orange accents for Halloween. Noelle's will be red and green for Christmas. Sweetie, yours is pink and red for Valentine's Day. Cloe's is green for Saint Patrick's."

Jesse butted in. "Liberty's is a firework show of color." He winked at her. "Because my gal is like a firework. Brilliant and stunning."

Liberty laughed. "You left out explosive." She looked at Belle and smiled brightly. "And yours, Belly, is going to be a patriotic red, white, and blue."

Belle didn't look impressed. She looked as

annoyed with the bed-and-breakfast idea as Corbin.

After her shower, she'd pulled her wet hair back in a ponytail and put on Wilder Wildcats sweats that he remembered her wearing in high school. Unlike her sister, Belle had never worn short skirts to show off her long legs. Or tight shirts and sweaters to define her full breasts. She'd never worn a lot of makeup to emphasize her green eyes or draw attention to her full lips. She'd been the quiet twin who seemed happy to live in her sister's shadow.

Which made him even more positive that the twin switch hadn't been her idea. She was just lying to cover Liberty's lie. A lie Liberty continued to perpetuate. She had convinced Jesse she knew nothing about a twin switch and Jesse had fallen for it.

But Corbin knew the truth. He blamed both twins for the deception. Liberty for coming up with the plan and Belle for executing it.

Although he blamed Belle the most.

She had borne witness to the infatuated fool who had showed up at her door all spit polished and holding a bouquet of thorny red roses he'd pilfered from Mrs. Stokes's garden. The fool who tripped over his feet as he walked her to the truck Mr. Crawley had loaned him for his "big date." The fool who didn't realize he had been duped until the date was over.

He had told Belle he'd figured the farce out right away and only stayed on the date because he'd wanted to see how far she'd go. But that was a lie. The truth was he'd been so wrapped up in his dream of dating Liberty that he hadn't known about the switch until after Belle had gone inside—after she had beguiled him with her lemony scent, her contagious laughter, and her mind-altering kisses.

As he stood there feeling happier than he'd ever felt in his life, Darla Holiday's voice had drifted out the window.

"You didn't tell me you had a date, Belle Justine. Who is that young man?"

"No one, Mama," Belle had answered. "Just a boy."

Corbin's happiness had wilted like the single rose petal lying on the porch floor.

Yes, he blamed Belle the most.

Chapter Four

CORBIN WAS STARING at her again. All through dinner, whenever Belle glanced in his direction his icy blue eyes were focused on her . . . and shooting daggers. She couldn't blame him. She deserved his anger. Liberty might have broken their date, but Belle was the one who had made her sister's rejection worse instead of better.

The plan had been for Belle to answer the door and tell Corbin that Liberty was sick and couldn't go on their date. But just one look at his pressed shirt, the roses in his hand, and the vulnerable look in his eyes and her heart had broken. When he had mistaken her for Liberty, she had thought it would be less hurtful if she just pretended to be her sister. Being a naïve teenager, she hadn't thought her plan through.

She hadn't planned on enjoying being with Corbin.

He turned out to be different from the other boys Belle had dated. He hadn't been all wrapped up in sports or his looks or trying to get in her jeans. He'd been thoughtful and kind and listened intently when she spoke. He'd talked more than he had in school, about math and books and the old westerns he enjoyed. He was funny in a dry wit kind of way that took her by surprise. Time had flown by. When he'd walked her to the door and looked at her with those cobalt-blue eyes, she'd forgotten it wasn't her he liked and had leaned in and kissed him.

And not just once.

On that warm night in May, they had stood on the porch and kissed repeatedly until she felt as weak as a newborn calf. She would have kept kissing him all night if Mama hadn't flashed the porch light. And it was a good thing her mama had. Corbin hadn't wanted to kiss Belle. He'd only wanted to see how far she'd go to try and convince him she was Liberty.

"He's a handsome man . . . if not a little angry."

Mimi's words startled Belle out of her thoughts and she realized she was staring at Corbin. The icy disdain was still there. She pulled her gaze away and turned to her grandmother.

"Keep your voice down, Mimi."

"He can't hear me all the way at the other end of the table." Mimi's eyes twinkled. "Which doesn't explain why he keeps staring down here at you. Did something happen in the barn?"

"Nothing, besides him letting me know in no uncertain terms that he has no intentions of giving back the ranch."

"Then it's a good thing we have a plan."

Belle stared at her. "A plan? What kind of plan?" It was never good when Mimi came up with plans. Her last plan to save the ranch had been marrying off one of her granddaughters to a Remington. Which hadn't saved the ranch at all. "I hope you don't think one of your granddaughters is going to marry Corbin because that's not going to happen."

Mimi chuckled. "Of course not. But it wouldn't hurt for you to become Corbin's friend."

"Is that why you, Mama, and Daddy haven't moved out yet? You're hoping to become Corbin's friends so he'll let Rome buy the ranch? Because that's not going to work, Mimi. Corbin doesn't want a Holiday as a friend."

Mimi got the stubborn look on her face she always got when she was determined to see something through. "Maybe he thinks he doesn't, but he just doesn't realize what good friends we Holidays make." She raised her voice. "Hey, Darla! Cut Corbin a piece of that pie you baked this mornin'."

Corbin certainly seemed to enjoy the pie. He didn't leave a buttery flake or cherry on his plate. Or maybe eating gave him something to do since he didn't seem to want to participate in the conversation. He spoke when asked a direct question, but other than that he didn't speak at all. She remembered him being quiet in high school as well. Which was why she'd been so surprised on their date. After a few awkward moments, he had opened up and become a completely different person. Belle couldn't help wondering if that person was still inside somewhere.

Not that she would find out. She wasn't about to do what her grandmother asked. Corbin didn't want her as a friend, and to be honest, she didn't want him as one either. He wasn't the same sweet boy she remembered. He was a vengeful man she wanted no part of. As far as she was concerned, it would be best if her family just accepted they were losing the ranch and moved out. She planned to tell her sisters just that at the next Secret Sisterhood meeting.

Her thoughts about Corbin and the ranch were interrupted when Liberty and Jesse got to their feet.

"Now that we're all finished with dessert," Liberty said. "Jesse and I want to tell you about our surprise. But first, I need to get Noelle and Hallie on the phone."

A few seconds later, Hallie's voice came through the speaker of Liberty's phone.

Loud and clear.

"Hey, Libby! I hope you're calling to tell me that the lowdown snake Corbin Whitlock is giving us back our ranch."

Everyone at the table cringed. Everyone but Jesse and Sunny who both threw back their heads and laughed.

"Nope," Sunny said in between snorts of laughter. "The lowdown snake and his sister are still here."

"Damn," Hallie grumbled. "Thanks for the warning, Libby."

Liberty rolled her eyes. "If you had given me a chance, I would have told you that everyone is here." She glanced at Sunny and Corbin. "Forgive my outspoken sister. But Hallie talks smack about everyone. Including her family. And pretty soon you and Sunny are going to be part of that family." She exchanged smiles with Jesse before she held out her hand to display the ruby ring on her finger. "Jesse and I are getting married!"

The entire room erupted with congratulations and the sound of chairs scraping back as everyone got up to offer hugs and handshakes to the happy couple.

Everyone but Belle.

She couldn't move. She was too stunned.

Married? Liberty was getting married? Belle felt like she was going to pass out. Or throw up. And not wanting to do either in front of everyone, she got to her feet and quietly slipped out the back door.

The storm had moved through, all that remained of it was a smattering of dark clouds on the eastern horizon. On the western, a brilliant sunset stretched its reddish-orange rays across the sky. Belle leaned back against the side of the house and took deep gulping breaths.

This wasn't right. Not right at all. Liberty had never wanted to get married. She wanted to run a successful business and make loads of money and grow old in a Galveston beach house. With Belle. Not Jesse.

The door opened and Liberty stepped out.

Belle had always gone along with every plan her sister had ever come up with, but she couldn't go along with this one. "What are you thinking, Libby?"

Liberty shrugged as she joined Belle. "Believe

me, I'm just as surprised as you are. I never thought I'd be one of those sappy women to fall head over heels for a man." A dreamy look spread over her face. "But I love him, Belly. I love him so much it hurts. When he got down on one knee last Saturday, this overwhelming joy at just the thought of spending the rest of my life with him hit me and I couldn't say no . . . I didn't want to say no."

Belle stared at her sister. "Last Saturday? You've known for over a week and you didn't say a word?"

"I thought it would be better to tell you in person."

"You could've come to Houston. It's not that far away."

"There's a lot going on with the renovations at the bed-and-breakfast. Jesse needed to be here."

"And you couldn't come without him? What happened to my sister who claimed she would never become one of those women who couldn't do anything without a man?"

Liberty smiled sheepishly. "I fell in love. And just to be clear, I can do things without Jesse. I came to help you pack up our business, didn't I? It's just that being apart from Jesse for too long is like missing half of my heart."

Belle felt like she'd been punched hard in the stomach and couldn't catch her breath. It was Liberty and Belle who were two halves of a whole. The ones who couldn't be apart. Their names said it all. Liberty Belle. Liberty Jesse didn't even go together. They hadn't shared a womb. The same crib. The same bottles and pacifiers. They weren't sisters who could finish each other's sentences. Or a team that complemented each other perfectly.

Whether it was the decorations for the homecoming dance or the Halloween costumes they wore for trick-or-treating, everything they did together turned out spectacular. Liberty was the vivacious decision maker and Belle was the soft-spoken worker bee. Liberty sketched out the plan and Belle brought it to life. Liberty saw the big picture and Belle took care of all the little details to make that picture a reality.

Which was why Holiday Sisters Events was so successful.

Liberty and Belle were the dream team.

Jesse didn't complement Liberty. They were too much alike. According to what she'd learned about him from family members, he was as much of a leader as her sister. There was no way he and Liberty could ever work as a team. Leaders needed followers.

What kind of a spell had Jesse placed on her sister? Liberty had never based any of her decisions on a man. In fact, she had barely dated after college. Her entire focus had been on making their business a success. Now her entire focus was on Jesse. In the last week, she had barely mentioned their upcoming events when she'd called. All she'd talked about was Jesse and his ridiculous idea to turn a house of ill repute into a bed-and-breakfast.

"I know you're upset, Belly," Liberty said.

That was the thing about being a twin. You couldn't hide anything from your sister. Or at least Belle couldn't hide anything from Liberty. Obviously, Liberty had been hiding a lot from her. Belle had thought Jesse was just a spring fling. Someone Liberty would get over. She had never thought her sister would marry him. She had never thought he would become Liberty's other half.

Liberty pulled her into her arms. "I'm sorry, Belly. You're right. I should have come to Houston and told you in person. I guess I've just been feeling as broadsided by everything as you do. My plans never included falling in love. But I promise you that Jesse is not going to come between us." But that was a lie. Jesse had already come between them. As if reading her thoughts, Liberty continued. "I swear, Belly. Just because I'm getting married in July that's not going to change what we have."

Belle drew back. "July? This July?"

Liberty sent her a sheepish look. "Jesse doesn't want to wait and we've always planned on getting married on the Fourth of July."

"We planned it. You and I planned to get married in a double ceremony on the Fourth of July."

"I know, Belly. But you're not getting married."

Belle's temper flared. "You shouldn't be either! I've gone along with every idea you have ever come up, Libby. Even the bad ones like stealing Daddy's truck when we were only fourteen and tearing up the Remingtons' alfalfa field. And sneaking into the boys' locker room and painting

Girls Rule in lipstick on their mirrors. But I'm not going along with this one. I won't stand by and let you make a mistake that could ruin your life forever. I won't do it, Libby. I know you think you love Jesse, but no one can love a man they barely know. I get that Sweetie and Cloe married quickly, but they have known Decker and Rome for most of their lives. You've only known Jesse a few months."

Liberty smiled softly. "It doesn't feel that way. It feels like I've known him forever." She hesitated. "You might not think I should marry Jesse, Belly, but I'm doing it."

Belle knew if she opened her mouth bad things would come out. As angry as she was, she didn't want to sling hurtful words that would put an even bigger chasm between her and her twin. She also knew her sister well enough to know that no matter what she said it wouldn't change Liberty's mind. In fact, like Mimi, the more you argued with Liberty, the more she dug her feet in. For now, it was best if Belle went along with her until she could come up with a plan. And she would. She wasn't about to let her sister get married to a man she barely knew.

"Then I guess there's nothing to say but congratulations."

Liberty hugged her close. "Thank you, Belly. I know you're going to need some time to get used to the idea, but I know you're going to love Jesse when you get to know him." She drew back. "Now let's go inside. Mimi popped open a bottle of her elderberry wine."

Belle shook her head. "I just need a minute."

"Belly—"

"No, really, I'm fine."

Liberty studied her for a moment before she nodded. "Okay."

After she was gone, Belle stood there watching the sun sink beneath the horizon and trying to come to grips with how quickly everything had changed. She had never been the type of person who liked change and now her entire life was spinning out of control and she couldn't seem to stop it.

"I take it you're not real happy about your sister and my brother's upcoming nuptials."

She startled and turned to see Corbin leaning against the corner of the house. He held out the glass in his hand. "I have strict orders from Mimi to deliver this. She thinks you might need it."

Since she could use a stiff drink, Belle took the glass and guzzled the wine like water. The strong, sweet elderberry wine slid easily down her throat and warmed her belly.

"Careful," Corbin said. "I've only had two glasses of your grandma's wine and I'm feeling like I drank half a bottle of tequila."

"I'm used to it. I grew up on elderberry wine." She set the empty glass on the back door stoop.

"You were allowed to drink wine as kids?"

"I wouldn't say allowed."

He laughed. Since it was the first time she'd seen him laugh since their date, she figured he must be tipsy. Just not tipsy enough to let her get away with not answering his question.

"So why aren't you happy about Jesse and Liberty getting married?"

It was one thing to tell her sister about how she felt. It was another to tell Jesse's brother—and the man foreclosing on the ranch. She pinned on a smile. "I'm happy. I just couldn't sit anymore. I'm still sore from the fall."

He wore a cowboy hat so she couldn't see his eyes, but she could feel them. "You're a horrible liar. You looked like you wanted to throw up when Liberty gave us the news." He studied the sunset. "And I'm not real happy about your sister marrying my brother either. But I don't think we have anything to worry about. I give them a few weeks at the most."

"And what makes you think that?"

"They're both too bossy and opinionated to live together without killing each other."

Since it was an accurate description of her sister, she couldn't help laughing. He didn't join in, but he did smile. She had forgotten how nice his smile was. He had smiled a lot on their date.

"When did you realize I wasn't Liberty?" she asked.

His smile faded. "Not soon enough. If I had been paying closer attention instead of walking around with my head in the clouds because I'd gotten a date with Liberty Holiday, I would have figured it out much sooner."

She stared at him. "How?"

He stepped closer, and she couldn't help taking a step back. His eyes matched the color of the dusky sky behind him as he reached out and brushed a finger over the bridge of her nose.

"You have freckles."

His touch caused heat to spiral through her and her voice didn't sound like her own when she spoke. "Liberty has freckles."

He studied her nose as if counting them. "Not as many as you do." His gaze lifted. "And then there's this." He touched the corner of her left eyebrow. Again a wave of heat rolled through her. Damn Mimi and her strong winemaking. "Where did you get this tiny scar?"

"I fell and hit my head on the corner of the coffee table when I was three."

"You seem to fall a lot." Before she could argue the point, he squinted, emphasizing his long dark lashes. "And your eyes are two different colors."

She blinked. "They are not?"

"They are too." He leaned closer. So close she could see her reflection in the deep blue of his eyes and feel his warm breath brush her cheeks. It smelled like sweet cherry pie and potent elderberry wine. The mixture was intoxicating. "The right one is definitely a slightly darker shade of Kelly green."

"That's not possible. I would know if my eyes were different shades."

"So I guess you don't know about the bow of your lips either." His gaze lowered to her mouth and heat didn't just roll through her. It settled low in her body, causing the spot between her legs to simmer like the thick gravy of Mama's chicken and dumplings. Her words came out stuttered, breathy, and low.

"W-W-What's wrong with the bow of my lips?"

"It's uneven." The pad of his finger touched the corner of her mouth and lightly traced its way up her top lip. "Yep." This time, his voice was low and breathy. "Definitely uneven." His finger didn't stop. When it reached the opposite corner, it turned and slowly swept over her bottom lip, pressing just enough that it entered her mouth and brushed the edge of her lower teeth.

Her heart seemed to stop as her breath sucked in.

They stood like that for what felt like forever. His cherry/elderberry breath warming her face. His cobalt-blue eyes taking up her entire view. And his pressing finger touching more than just her lip.

Then suddenly as if a switch had been flipped, Corbin's hand dropped and he stepped away. "We better get back inside."

She wasn't ready to go back inside ... especially when she felt like a puddle of melted butter. But she wasn't about to say that when Corbin looked so unaffected. As she moved toward the back door, she realized Corbin had succeeded in one thing.

He'd taken her mind off Liberty getting married.

Chapter Five

"I DIDN'T ASK FOR a horse." Corbin stared at the horse Jesse had just backed out of the trailer. The beast was huge, solid black, and scary looking as hell.

Jesse grinned from ear to ear. "If you're going to be a rancher, Whitty, you're going to need to learn how to ride. In order to ride, you need to have a horse." He stroked the horse's forehead and the animal jerked his head away. "This here is Damian."

"As in the satanic kid in that horror movie?"

Jesse's brow knitted. "Hmm? I don't believe I saw that one. But if you don't like his name you can change it. How about Homer?"

"That horse looks like a Homer as much as Satan looks like an angel."

"I believe Satan was an angel," Sunny piped up. "Just a fallen one." She stood with the horse Jesse had brought her, stroking its shiny brown coat and looking like she was about to bust from happiness. Corbin should have bought her a horse—one much smaller than the one she was fawning over—and he was a little miffed that he hadn't thought of it. "How about Oreo?" she said.

"I'm not riding a horse named Oreo."

"Then Homer it is." Jesse grinned brightly. "Now let's get him saddled up so we can start your first lesson, Whitty."

Corbin stared at the horse that was snorting and pulling at the reins Jesse held. "Today?"

"Don't tell me you have other plans. Mimi told Liberty when she called this morning that you were cussing up a storm because you can't get anyone out to fix the Wi-Fi. Without Wi-Fi, you can't get much work done."

"I have plenty of work that doesn't need Wi-Fi. And I was not cussing up a storm." He'd only gotten out a few choice words before Mimi had scolded him for using bad language. She'd also scolded him for not pulling out Sunny's chair at breakfast and for carrying Tay around too much and not giving her enough space to be a cat.

Which was why Tay wasn't in his arms where she belonged. He wasn't happy about it. Not happy at all. If Mimi wasn't bossing him around, Hank was trying to teach him how to fix a chicken coop or replace shingles on the roof or muck out a stall. He hadn't realized how many jobs there were to do on a ranch that had nothing to do with being a cool cowboy.

Clint Eastwood wouldn't be caught dead shoveling horse poop.

"Come on, Whitty," Jesse said. "Riding isn't that bad. As an ex-rodeo roper, I know my way around horses. I promise I won't let you get hurt . . . too much. Falling off is just part of riding."

The memory of Belle flying off the back of the horse had Corbin's stomach knotting. But he couldn't back down. Not when owning a ranch had been all his idea.

It had been a bad one.

He figured that out after he settled into Homer's saddle and realized how far it was from the ground.

"Now see. That wasn't so hard, was it?" Jesse stood in front of the horse, holding the reins. "We're going to start out with a nice easy walk around the paddock."

Start out? As far as Corbin was concerned, a nice easy walk around the paddock was all he planned to do today. Sunny had other plans. While he was getting the hang of walking the horse around the paddock—with Jesse right beside him on the big bay horse that had been in the barn—Sunny was practicing riding her horse in the field behind the barn.

It looked like she didn't need practice. She had gotten much more accomplished since the horseback riding excursion she and Corbin had gone on when she was in college. Watching her gallop across a field that was no doubt filled with potholes and gopher holes, at a neck-breaking pace, scared the hell out of him.

"Go stop her, Jesse," he said. "Now."

"She's fine, Whitty. It looks like she got the family knack with horses." Jesse lifted an eyebrow. "Some of the family."

Corbin glared at him. "Very funny."

Jesse laughed. "Lighten up. I'm teasing. You're doing great and ready to brave the wilds." He opened the gate.

Corbin shook his head. "I'm not ready."

"Of course you are. Just loosen your grip on the reins a little and quit sitting in the saddle like a stiff poker. If you can stare down a hard-ass business mogul and get his money to invest, you can handle riding a horse."

"I'd rather stare down a hard-ass mogul," he said as the horse walked out of the paddock.

Jesse followed and moved up next to him. "Then why are you here? Why aren't you back in your office in Houston?"

"I told you. This is all for Sunny."

Jesse studied him for a long moment. Corbin knew Jesse was torn between wanting Liberty's family to keep their ranch and wanting his new sister to be happy. While Corbin and Jesse had met almost three years ago, Jesse and Sunny had just met a month ago. Still, it was easy to see the bond between them. They looked like their daddy while Corbin looked more like his and Sunny's mother.

It hadn't been a surprise that Daddy had fooled around with another woman and gotten her pregnant. Or that the woman had turned out to be a child abuser and the state had taken Jesse away from her. Daddy had never gone for motherly women. What had been surprising was that Jesse had been adopted by one of the wealthiest families in Texas and had still come looking for his half brother and sister. And not just looking for them, but wanting a relationship with them.

Corbin had tried blowing him off. He hadn't wanted anything to do with his brother by another mother. But Jesse had refused to give up. No matter how many times Corbin ignored his calls and texts, Jesse kept right on calling and texting. He'd shown up at Corbin's work and offered advice. He followed him to bars and bought him drinks. When Corbin had told him about his dream to start his own investment company, Jesse had offered to stake him. Still, thanks to his parents' desertion, it had taken Corbin a long time before he completely trusted Jesse.

He trusted him now.

Jesse trusted him too.

He smiled his big dopey smile. "Well, if this ranch is what Sunny wants, then this ranch is what Sunny will get." He glanced over to where their sister was riding in circles. "Hey, Sunny! I'm heading over to Rome's to help with branding, you want to come?"

Before Corbin could get after Jesse for making the offer, Sunny yelled back. "Hell yeah, I do! I'll race you to the Remingtons'." With a loud "Yeehaw!" she took off across the pasture.

Jesse laughed. "I better go after her so she doesn't get lost." He took off and called over his shoulder. "Just take Homer back into the barn and I'll unsaddle him later."

Unfortunately, Homer had other ideas . . . like joining the fun and chasing after Jesse's and Sunny's horses. Corbin had to hang on for dear life or end up in the dirt. It took him a good while to get the horse to slow down. When Homer finally came to a stop, Corbin realized two things. Sunny and Jesse were nowhere in sight and he didn't have a clue where he was.

Cussing out his siblings, he took out his phone and tried pulling up GPS. For some reason, it wasn't working. Probably the same reason he couldn't get Wi-Fi at the house. He was living in a dead zone.

And a hot zone.

The temperature had to be in the high nineties already and it wasn't even noon yet. If Homer didn't decide to toss him off and break his neck, he was going to die of thirst and heat exposure. Not that Homer looked like he was about to buck him off. In fact, he seemed as drained by the heat as Corbin and was plodding along as if the next step would be his last.

Did horses drop dead from heat?

Corbin had a lot of pride. If it had just been him wandering around in the heat, he would have kept going—even if they found his skeleton remains years later. But he wasn't about to let his pride kill a horse. He guided Homer over to the shade of a mesquite tree, dismounted, and called Sunny.

She answered right away. "Geez, Cory, I'm fine. So stop worrying about me. I'm not going to get a big Y branded over my heart. I'm just standing on the fence watching. You should see how efficient this is. Rome, Casey, and their crew have already inoculated, tagged, and branded like fifty cows. It's unbelievable ... and sexy as hell. I might just have to marry me a cowboy. I'm thinking Casey Remington might do."

"You're not getting married until you're older. And while you've been gawking at Casey, Homer and I have been wandering around lost."

There was a long pause. "Wait a second. You followed us? Jesse and I thought you stayed back at the ranch."

"I wanted to, but Homer had other ideas."

A burst of laughter came through the receiver before Sunny yelled. "Hey, Jesse, you're not going to believe this, but Corbin followed us and is now lost." More laughter before Jesse came on.

"Hey, Whitty! So you're lost, huh?" The smirk in his voice was extremely annoying.

"I'm sure you two are real amused. But you won't be if this horse drops dead of thirst and heat." Jesse snorted with laughter and Corbin scowled. "It's not funny, Jess. Get me some water and a trailer for this horse and get it now!"

"Don't freak out, Whitty. Where are you?"

"If I knew that, I wouldn't be lost, now would I?"

"Look around. Are there any distinguishing landmarks?"

Corbin glanced around. "A bunch of rocks and mesquite trees, a dead gnarled oak tree that looks like it's flipping me off—shit, is that a horse skull?"

"I'm sure it's a mule deer skull."

"And that's better?"

Jesse laughed, but quickly sobered. "Okay. You

have to be somewhere from here to the Holiday Ranch. I don't know the area very well, but I'm sure I can find someone who does and can tell me where the fuck-you tree is. Although most of those folks are pretty busy right now—wait, there's Belle and Cloe."

"Don't—" Before Corbin could finish, Jesse hung up.

"Dammit!" he yelled up at the clear blue sky. The last person he wanted to know he was lost was Belle Holiday. And he didn't know why. What difference did it make if she knew he was inept at finding his way from one ranch to another? He didn't care what she thought.

But a good twenty minutes later, he couldn't stop the rush of embarrassment that flooded his body when he realized who was driving the pickup truck headed toward him.

The Remington Ranch truck stopped only feet away and Belle hopped out. She was dressed like she had been yesterday when she was tossed off the horse. A T-shirt, jeans, and roper boots. But this time, her T-shirt wasn't white, soaking wet, and see through. It was pink and no doubt matched the blush on his cheeks. Which made him snappish.

"What are you doing here? Jesse was supposed to come."

If his rudeness bothered her, she didn't let on. "He and Sunny wanted to finish watching the branding. And since I knew exactly where you were, I volunteered." She moved to the back of the truck and pulled down the tailgate. When he saw her struggling with a large white container of water, he hurried over to help. Their hands brushed as he took it from her and heat speared through him at the mere touch of her cool skin.

Maybe he had heatstroke. It seemed like the only logical explanation.

He quickly took it from her and then almost dropped it when he turned and saw Homer standing right behind him. Belle didn't comment on his fear of the horse, but there was a slight smile on her lips.

Lips that had completely screwed with his mind the night before.

Of course, it hadn't been her lips as much as Mimi's strong elderberry wine that had him seconds from kissing Belle.

At least, that's what he kept telling himself.

"Pour some water in here," Belle said as she snapped open what looked like a round canvas tote. Corbin unscrewed the cap from the container and tipped water into the tote. He expected Homer to dive in and start drinking. Instead, the horse just stood there.

"Drink up, Homer," he said.

"Homer?" Belle reached out and stroked the horse's neck. "You don't look like a Homer. And it doesn't look like you're thirsty either." She glanced at Corbin. "Horses can go a long time without water."

"How exactly was I supposed to know that? He was plodding along like he was on his last leg."

"Horses are extremely intuitive. He was probably taking his cues from you and knew you didn't like going fast."

"I wish he had figured that out before he took off after Jesse and Sunny and almost dumped me on my head."

A smile tickled the corners of her mouth again. A mouth he had trouble keeping his gaze from. "I would have liked to see that."

He scowled. "I'm sure you would have."

"You shouldn't let it hurt your pride. I've been on runaway horses numerous times." She reached into the cooler in the bed of the truck and pulled out a bottle of water. He gratefully accepted it. Homer might not be thirsty, but he certainly was.

"Thanks." He unscrewed the lid and guzzled most of it before he lowered the bottle to find Belle watching him with the same look she had given him last night when his finger was pressed against her lip. Last night, he had blamed it on the wine. Today, he didn't know what to blame it on. Belle wasn't sexually interested in him.

Was she?

He mentally shook the thought from his head and returned to their conversation. "And not being able to control a runaway horse didn't hurt your pride?"

"Control and pride aren't really my flaws. They're Liberty's."

"And what are yours?"

She hesitated for a moment before she spoke. "Bad decisions."

"I'm not sure I understand. What kind of bad decisions are we talking about?"

"All the decisions I make without help are usually bad. Grocery store lines, clothing, hairstyles, ice cream flavors."

He stared at her. "How can you make a bad decision about ice cream? I don't think I've ever met an ice cream I didn't like."

"Have you ever tasted licorice ice cream?"

He squinted. "You actually ordered licorice ice cream?"

"I love licorice so I thought I'd like it in ice cream. It turns out some flavors are just not meant to be mixed with cream."

"True, but you never know until you try. And that wasn't a bad decision. It was just a test. It might have turned out to be your favorite ice cream of all time."

She scrunched up her face. "Licorice?"

He didn't want to find this woman cute, but damned if he couldn't help laughing. "You're right. The odds were against you, but it's still not what I would call a bad decision. Now, allowing your brother to talk you into riding a wild-eyed beast is a bad decision." Homer chose that moment to come up and nudge his shoulder. He tentatively stroked the horse's soft forehead. When he glanced over, Belle was smiling.

"You don't look too upset about riding that wild beast."

He shrugged. "It wasn't as bad as I thought. So how did you know where to find me?"

She glanced at the gnarled tree. "As kids, it was my and Liberty's secret place that none of our other sisters knew about. We even hid a time capsule in the hollow trunk when we were thirteen. We planned to come back and take it out when we both turned thirty." Her eyes grew sad. "But I'm sure she's forgotten all about it now."

After what she'd done to him, he didn't think he'd ever feel sympathy for her, but he'd been wrong. He knew what it was like to love your sibling above all else. Sunny was the only one who was always there for him. The only one he could count on no matter what. He'd come to love Jesse, but he still didn't love him like he loved his sister. He and Sunny were connected by more than just blood. They were connected by the things they'd lived through.

It looked like Belle and Liberty were the same.

"I'm sure she hasn't forgotten the tree or your time capsule," he said. "She's just a little consumed with Jesse right now. It won't last. Jesse's smart. He'll figure it out."

Belle stared at him. "Figure what out?"

"That Liberty isn't who he thinks she is."

Her eyes flared with temper. He was surprised. He'd never thought of her as the fiery one. "And just what does that mean? If anyone will figure it out, it will be Liberty. From what I've heard, Jesse is nothing but a wandering rodeo bum who can't stay in one place long enough to get a mailing address."

"I wouldn't call a multi-millionaire a rodeo bum, but you're right about Jesse not staying in one place for very long. Which is another reason I'm convinced it won't last."

"So you think Jesse is just going to take off one day and leave my sister with a broken heart?"

"I think it's as possible as your sister changing her mind and breaking Jesse's heart." He cocked a brow. "Something I have personal experience with. And why do you look so upset? Isn't that what you're hoping for? You're hoping they'll break up so you can have your sister all to yourself."

Belle opened her mouth as if to argue, but then slowly closed it. Her deflated look bothered him for some reason and he found himself softening his voice. "Look, I get it. You love her and you don't want to lose her."

She glanced at him. "Is that why you wanted our ranch? You thought it was a way to keep Sunny close to you?"

He should have left it at that. Belle didn't deserve his truth. But for some reason, he gave it to her anyway. "I want Sunny to have it all—a husband, a family, a happily-ever-after. Once she does, I'll be content to fade into the background."

Belle's mismatched eyes seemed to drill right through him. "What about you? Don't you want a happily-ever-after?"

He had once. Once he'd dreamed about a ranch and a wife and a passel of dark-haired daughters. But it had been a foolish dream. Now, he was anything but foolish.

"I've learned it's best not to want too much. That way you're never disappointed when you don't get it."

Chapter Six

"BEFORE WE GET to the reason Belle called this meeting," Cloe said. "I just want to make it clear I don't think it's right that Liberty's not here."

Belle was feeling guilty about it too. This was the first meeting of the Holiday Secret Sisterhood Liberty hadn't attended. Belle was the reason she wasn't there. She had asked her sisters to keep the meeting a secret from Liberty. She felt like she was stabbing her sister in the back, but sometimes you had to exclude a sister to save a sister.

Something Hallie had no trouble pointing out.

"We met without Sweetie when we worried about her being depressed about not making it as a country singer." Her voice blared through the speaker of Cloe's laptop. Hallie and Noelle were on Zoom while Sweetie, Belle, and Cloe were sitting in the kitchen at the Remington Ranch.

"And I was extremely hurt about that." Sweetie took a big bite of the coffee cake Cloe had served them. Pregnancy had greatly improved her appetite. She had taken "eating for two" to a whole new level. She waved her fork at the laptop screen Hallie and Noelle peered from. "And I still am."

"Well, don't point at me," Noelle said. "It wasn't my idea. I don't call the meetings. I just show up for them—even when I don't have the time. So, Belly, get to the point of this one so I can get back to studying for my pastry exam." Noelle took cooking seriously and was one of the top students at her culinary school in Dallas. She had big plans to open up her own bakery one day and be a major social media influencer. Since she had as much tenacity and drive as Liberty, Belle knew she would succeed . . . if she didn't get mixed up with some guy and lose her ability to think clearly.

"I'm worried Liberty is making a big mistake marrying Jesse," Belle said. "And we need to do something to stop it."

She expected her sisters to jump in and agree and was surprised when they didn't. Cloe and Sweetie exchanged looks, but didn't say a word. Neither did Noelle and Hallie.

Belle swept her gaze around. "Don't tell me no one else thinks it's crazy that Liberty is planning on marrying a man she's only known for a couple months in just a little over a month."

"I didn't really know Rome," Cloe said.

"Yes, you did. He's been our neighbor all our lives."

Hallie spoke up. "A neighbor we never hung out with because his daddy was our daddy's archenemy. And still is."

"Would you keep it down?" Cloe glanced around. "And Sam and Daddy aren't archenemies now that Rome and I are married."

Hallie snorted. "You keep believin' that, sis. But I saw the way they were looking at each other at y'all's wedding. If they had been carrying guns, it would have been gunfight at the OK Corral all over again."

Noelle, who had always had an ongoing feud with the youngest Remington, jumped in. "I would certainly have drawn a gun on Casey if I'd had one when he pushed me into Sweetie's wedding cake."

"Casey pushed you into Sweetie's cake?" Cloe said. "I thought you tripped."

"I didn't want to tell you the truth when you married that jerk's brother. But I don't know how you live in the same house with Casey."

Cloe smiled. "Casey is a sweetheart, Elle. You just haven't gotten a chance to know him. He built me the cutest cradle. I can't wait to see how it looks in the baby's room."

Belle couldn't help wondering why Cloe hadn't shown her the cradle or the baby's room. But they were getting off topic.

"We can't let Liberty get her heart broken and I know that's what's going to happen. Even Corbin said Jesse is a rolling stone and will be ready to move on soon."

Sweetie stopped eating and stared at her. "Corbin said that?"

"Not in so many words, but he agreed he didn't think Jesse would go through with the marriage.

After he intimated that Liberty would be the one to break Jesse's heart."

"I can see how he'd think that after Liberty broke the date with him," Cloe said.

This would probably be a good time to tell her sisters about the twin switch she'd pulled, but she didn't want to get the conversation off track. Nor did she want them letting it slip to Liberty. Her and her sister's relationship was already on shaky ground.

"Yes, Liberty broke a date with Corbin, but they weren't in a relationship. We all know Liberty is loyal to a fault. Once she loves you, she loves you for life. Which means if any hearts are going to be broken, it will be hers."

Belle wasn't about to let that happen, but it looked like her sisters didn't agree.

"I don't think Jesse is going to break her heart," Cloe said. "Have you seen him with Liberty? He dotes on her."

"I'm sure he's doted on a lot of women. That's all part of his rodeo cowboy charm."

"There's something to that," Hallie said. "I've dated a few rodeo cowboys and it's like they have a book they share on how to make women drop their panties."

Noelle crinkled her nose. "Ooo, that's gross, Hal."

"Just speaking the truth."

"Speaking of the truth." Cloe looked at Belle with concerned eyes. "Are you sure your dislike of Jesse isn't based on . . . something else?"

"I think she's trying to ask you if you're jealous

of Jesse and Liberty's relationship, Belly," Hallie clarified.

"I'm not going to deny I feel a little slighted by Liberty's infatuation with Jesse, but if I thought Jesse would make her happy, y'all know I wouldn't have called this meeting. I'm seriously concerned. Liberty isn't acting at all like herself."

Sweetie reached across the table and squeezed her hand. "She's in love, Belle. Love changes things."

But it shouldn't. It shouldn't change things. Especially between sisters. But the looks on Sweetie's and Cloe's faces kept Belle from saying that. They thought she was just jealous. And she was. But she was also concerned.

"Y'all know Liberty. When she wants something, she goes after it with both guns blazing. That's fine in business, but it's not fine in love. She needs to slow down and think about what she's doing—and who she's doing it with—before she ends up getting hurt."

Sweetie sighed. "Okay, Belly. I'll talk with her. But I'm not going to bad mouth Jesse. I like him."

"I do too," Cloe said. "I think you will too, Belly, once you get to know him."

Belle disagreed, but again she kept her mouth shut. Obviously, Jesse had charmed her sisters as well as Liberty. But he wasn't going to charm her.

"I get that you're worried, Belly," Noelle said. "But if anyone can take care of herself, it's Libby."

"Elle does have a good point." Hallie hopped in. "Liberty is one tough nut. I'm sure she'll be fine. Now how are things going at convincing that no-account ranch thief to sell the ranch to Rome? Liberty acted like she had some kind of a plan, but wouldn't tell me what it was. Did she tell you?"

Belle bristled. "A plan? She didn't tell me anything about a plan. But she doesn't seem to tell me anything these days. And if she has a plan, she's certainly not implementing it. She's too busy with Jesse's harebrained idea of turning Mrs. Fields' into a bed-and-breakfast."

"I don't think that's a harebrained idea," Sweetie said. "The town needs a place for visitors to stay. Especially if y'all are moving your event business here. And Mimi mentioned a plan for saving the ranch too, but wouldn't go into detail."

"She seems to think that befriending Corbin will make him change his mind," Belle said. "But that isn't going to work. Corbin wants the ranch for Sunny and he loves his sister as much as we love each other."

"Then let the thieving asshole buy another ranch," Hallie fumed.

"He doesn't want another ranch. He has some image in his head of the Holiday Ranch being the perfect home for Sunny."

"For Sunny? Isn't he planning on living there too?" Cloe asked.

The stab of sympathy Belle had felt yesterday hit her again. *I've learned it's best not to want too much. That way you're never disappointed when you don't get it.* They had been such hopeless words that she'd had the overwhelming urge to pull Corbin into her arms and hug him. Which was silly. He didn't want hugs. Especially from a Holiday.

"I don't think he cares where he lives," she said. "Maybe because he's lived in so many places."

"It sounds like you've become friends with the enemy, Belly," Noelle said.

Hallie jumped in before Belle could answer. "It sure does. And maybe Mimi's idea isn't just a bad thing. You've always had a talent for getting people to open up and talk to you. Maybe you can get Corbin to confide in you and we can find the chink in his armor. Besides, it will give you something else to worry about besides you and Liberty not being joined at the hip anymore."

Belle scowled. "I don't expect Liberty to be joined at my hip. We spent the last month without each other and I did just fine."

"You weren't fine. Every time I called, you sounded like a lost calf that couldn't find her mama. Damn, Belly, you didn't think you and Libby were going to live together forever, did you?"

"Of course not." But she had thought they would live close to each other with husbands who never came between them. She had never imagined herself feeling like an outsider.

"Well, I wish I could say this has been a productive meeting," Noelle said. "But all I've gotten out of it is that Belly is jealous of Jesse and Corbin has no intentions of selling Rome back the ranch. So if that's all, I'm out." She waved before her side of the screen went blank. Hallie soon followed, leaving Cloe and Sweetie sitting there giving Belle a sympathetic look.

Before she could reiterate that she wasn't jealous of Jesse, just concerned for Liberty, Rome came in with an armload of skinny shipping boxes.

"I hate to interrupt, Lucky, but I think the wallpaper you ordered is here." He set the multiple boxes on the island and smiled at Cloe. "And I think you got plenty to cover, not only the baby's room, but also the entire house. Although Casey might throw a fit when he comes home and finds his room done in prancing ponies with pink bows."

Cloe laughed. "I bet he won't. He's as excited about the baby as your daddy is." She got up and walked into Rome's waiting arms. They kissed like Sweetie and Belle weren't there. When they drew back, Rome looked starry eyed and lovestruck.

"I'll paper the entire house in pink ponies for kisses like that. When do you want me to start putting it up in the baby's room?" Cloe must have sent Rome some kind of nonverbal message because he glanced over at Belle. "Oh, right. There's no hurry then. I'll just let you ladies get back to your meeting." He gave her another kiss before he left.

Belle didn't put two and two together until she'd left the Remington Ranch and was headed into town. The room Belle was staying in was going to be the baby's room. Which made sense when it was right next door to Cloe and Rome's room. That's why Cloe hadn't shown Belle the cradle and the baby's room. They couldn't start decorating it with Belle staying in it.

Talk about feeling like the odd person out. When she arrived at Mrs. Fields' Boardinghouse and found Jesse and Liberty kissing in front of the carriage house, the feeling only grew. But instead of staying in her car and giving them a few minutes of privacy, she got out and loudly slammed her door.

Jesse pulled away, but Liberty continued to cling to him like the wisteria vines that grew on the side of the carriage house.

"Hey, Belly!" Jesse sent her a big, toothy smile.

She scowled. "Only close family call me that."

Her rudeness caused Liberty to untangle herself from Jesse in a hurry. "Belly!"

Jesse didn't seem to be at all offended. "Now, Libby Lou, I remember when you didn't like me using your nickname either." He winked at Belle. "You're right. We need to get to know each other before we start using nicknames. How about if I give you a tour of your new office? Liberty has been chomping at the bit to see it. But since it's your office too, Belle, I made her wait until you could see it together."

Belle didn't want a tour from Jesse, but to decline really would be rude. Especially when Jesse was the one renting them the carriage house and at a low price. Which is why they had decided to move their business to Wilder. That, and they both wanted to be closer to their family. Belle hadn't realized Liberty pushing to move home also had to do with Jesse moving there. If she had known, she wouldn't have agreed.

But it was too late to do anything about it now. Their Houston office's lease was up and so was their apartment's. The moving van with all their furniture and office equipment would be there any day.

Although as it turned out, they wouldn't need any of their office furniture or equipment. It looked like Jesse had not only renovated the carriage house, but also decorated the loft that would serve as their office. An expensive-looking beige leather couch and chairs were in the waiting area, along with an antique credenza that held a coffee bar. In front of the floor-to-ceiling windows was a round white oak conference table with six cowhide chairs. The rest of the loft was dedicated to two office spaces with desks, new laptops, phones, and high-tech office chairs. The room to the left of the stairs led to a bathroom and the room at the back looked like it held a printer and small kitchenette.

"Surprise!" Jesse said with his big goofy grin.

Liberty released a squeal and dove into his arms while Belle just stood there in shock. This was nothing like their office in Houston. That office had been small with very few windows, stained carpeting, and a faulty air conditioner that worked only half of the time. This loft had plenty of windows, a rustic oak plank floor, and a constant flow of cool air that dried the sweat on the back of Belle's neck.

"So what do you think, Belle?" Jesse asked as

he tucked an arm around Liberty and pulled her close.

"It's fine. Thank you."

"Fine?" Liberty stared at her. "This is your dream office, Jelly Belly, and you know it."

"I don't think I dreamed about cowhide chairs." She knew she was being petty, but she couldn't seem to stop herself.

Liberty sighed. "You are really starting to annoy the crap out of me, Belle Holiday."

Usually this was the point when Belle backed down. But she was too angry and hurt to back down today.

"Well, then we're even because you have been annoying the crap out of me for weeks. You left me doing everything for the business while you were here kicking up your heels and signing us up to do numerous events for the folks of Wilder without even asking me. And to top everything off, your boyfriend decided to decorate our office without even considering my preferences."

Jesse cleared his throat. "I had a decorator from Austin do it and she said she can change anything you don't like. Just say the word."

"You won't change a thing!" Liberty glared at Belle. "It's perfect."

Belle glared back. "Oh, and if it's perfect for you, then that's all that matters. That's all that ever matters. If you think we should move to Houston and start an event-planning business, we move to Houston and start an event-planning business. If you think we should leave Houston and come back to Wilder, we leave everything we've worked so hard for and come back to Wilder. Whatever Liberty wants, Liberty gets."

Liberty's face turned bright red and Belle knew she had pushed the wrong button. Jesse knew it too.

"Now, honey, I'm sure your sister didn't—" He cut off when Liberty turned on him. He held up his hands. "I'll just let you two talk it out."

Once he was gone, Liberty looked back at Belle. "Do you know why I always make all the decisions, Belly? Because you're the most indecisive person I have ever met in my life. You can't decide what line to get in at the grocery store, you can't decide what flavor of ice cream you want at Baskin-Robbins, you can't decide what you want off a menu at a restaurant. And if you do finally decide, you're never happy with your choice. And it makes me so damn frustrated, I decide for you. But I would damn well love it if you could think for yourself, Belly. Then I wouldn't have had the added pressure of making you happy all my life!"

Belle fumed. "Making me happy? Tell that lie to someone else. All you think about is yourself, Libby. I wouldn't be standing here in this office if it wasn't for you. Now I know why you pushed so hard for us to move here. It had nothing to do with Jesse giving us a great deal on Mrs. Fields' carriage house. Or being centrally located. Or using the barn as a wedding venue. Or being closer to our family. It had to do with you having the hots for an ex-rodeo bum. Because that's all it is, Libby. No one falls in love after only a few weeks!"

"You're wrong, Belly. I am in love. But you're right about you not being here without me." She waved a hand around. "This is your dream, Belly. It was never mine. Do you think I wanted to be an event planner? I chose it because I knew how much you loved celebrating with people. Like Mama, you enjoy decorating for every holiday and throwing people big parties. I thought Belly would love to do that for the rest of her life. And now you're mad at me for trying to make your dream come true—for making the choice because you're too scared of failing to choose anything for yourself? Well, screw you, Belly! Screw you!"

Belle felt like the designer rug under her feet had just been yanked out from beneath her. Not by some unseen force, but by her own sister. With tears blurring her eyes, she headed for the stairs. She didn't know how she made it down them. Her legs felt like they had no bones and her hands were shaking so badly she dropped her car keys as soon as she pulled them out of her purse.

Before she could pick them up off the ground, Jesse did. When she straightened, his brown eyes were filled with sympathy and compassion.

"Maybe you need to take a few minutes before you get behind the wheel, Belle."

"So she's convinced you that I can't think for myself." She jerked the keys from him. "Well, I have news for both of you. I don't need anyone telling me what to do. I can manage just fine on my own!" She got into her car and started it before peeling out in a spray of gravel.

But her words were all lies.

As she drove down the long driveway, she didn't have a clue where she was going or what she was going to do.

Chapter Seven

Corbin slowed his brand-new dually truck down to thirty miles per hour as soon as he reached the outskirts of Wilder. As a teenager, he'd hated the speed limit. Now he didn't mind going slow so much. It gave him time to look around.

When he had left town after graduating, he'd thought he would never return. His ego had been badly stung by the Holiday twins and he'd had no desire to see them or the Podunk town ever again. Then Uncle Dan died and shockingly willed him and Sunny his old trailer and the land it sat on—no doubt because he'd felt guilty about his lack of care when Corbin and Sunny had been living with him. Corbin had planned to sell both the trailer and the land. But when he got ready to put them on the real estate market, something had stopped him.

He still wasn't sure what.

The trailer was a piece of junk and had been even when he and Sunny had lived there. The land was no more than a half acre of weed-infested dirt. He glanced around at the businesses that lined the one-block main street. His reluctance to sell certainly didn't have anything to do with this town. Wilder was as dull and boring as every other small Texas town.

And yet, there was some invisible thread that held him tethered. He and Sunny had lived in a lot of places and he cared nothing about seeing any of them again. But this town was different. Maybe it had to do with the townsfolk more than the town itself. He hadn't formed any bonds in the other places they'd lived, but here he'd had to form bonds. Uncle Dan hadn't been willing to spend any money on the brats living with him so Corbin had been forced to get jobs so Sunny could go to school looking like the other kids.

He'd washed coffee cups and muffin tins at Nothin' But Muffins. He'd bussed tables at the Hellhole restaurant and bar. He had swept up hair and cleaned sinks at both the barbershop and the salon. He had stocked shelves and waited on customers at Crawley's General Store. And he had run errands and been a general gopher for the owner of the town bank. At each job, he'd bonded with the owners: Sheryl Ann, Bobby Jay, Deb Haskins, Joe Marshall, Mr. Crawley, and Fiona Stokes.

Especially Mrs. Stokes.

While ornery and opinionated, the old woman had taken him under her wing and taught him as much as Jesse about money and how to make it. She was a little rough around the edges, but that's what he liked about her. She never pulled punches.

Which was one of the reasons he'd been avoiding her. Every time he saw her around town, he'd gone in the opposite direction. Like the rest of the townsfolk, he figured she wasn't happy about him foreclosing on the Holiday Ranch. But he couldn't keep avoiding her forever.

He pulled into a parking space in front of the bank and got out, wincing when his butt muscles protested. After all the riding he'd done the day before, it was an effort to put one foot in front of the other. He now understood how Belle had felt. And Homer hadn't even tossed him off.

As soon as he stepped inside the bank, he spotted Mrs. Stokes sitting behind her big maple desk in the back corner of the bank. Her hair was still dyed bright red and she still wore business suits that were fifty years outdated. On the coatrack behind her hung her ratty mink stole that she wore around town no matter the temperature outside. She glanced up, and he wasn't surprised when a stern frown settled over her wrinkled face.

"Well, if it isn't the town villain, Corbin Whiplash." She waved him over.

He complied and carefully eased down in the chair in front of her desk, thankful it had plenty of cushion. "Corbin Whiplash?"

"It's the new nickname the town has given you," she said. "Although I guess you're too young to remember the cartoon character Snidely Whiplash. Anyway, he was a villain who was always tying the heroine to train tracks . . . and trying to take her ranch."

She had taught him not to show any weakness when making business deals so he didn't apologize. "I didn't try," he said dryly. "I succeeded."

A smile lit her face, showing off her full set of dentures. He knew this because he'd seen them sitting in a glass once when he'd gone over to her big mansion to help her clean out the attic. It had scared the shit out of him. Of course, seeing her without the teeth had scared him even more.

She snorted. "You always were a cocky boy. It looks like you still are. And you're right. Business is business. If Hank Holiday was dumb enough to let his feud with Sam Remington make him land greedy, than he got what he deserved." She pulled a cigarette out of a pack sitting on her desk, but she didn't light it. She just placed it in her mouth and drew in deeply. "That's men for you. They think with their egos instead of their brains." She sent him a pointed look.

"Foreclosing on the ranch had nothing to do with my ego," he said. "Like I said, it was just business."

And Sunny.

Sunny was already settling into the Holiday Ranch as if she'd lived there all her life. He'd come downstairs that morning to find her in the kitchen with Darla learning how to make cinnamon rolls. Corbin usually didn't eat breakfast, but the warm cinnamon rolls drenched in icing were too hard to resist. After sneaking one from the tray, he'd headed to his office with Tay in tow. He'd intended to get some work done, but instead he'd been distracted by the view out his window of Sunny and Mimi working side by side in the garden. Later in the afternoon, he'd watched as Hank taught Sunny how to rope.

Uncle Dan had painted Hank Holiday out to be an arrogant asshole. After what the twins had done to him, Corbin had believed him. Now he realized he'd been wrong. Hank was gruff, but he was also a hardworking man who was patient and kind. He never once got frustrated when Sunny missed the fence post. He just readjusted the rope and had her try again.

As Corbin had watched his sister connect with the Holidays, he'd realized that Sunny would miss the Holidays as much as they would miss their ranch. Letting them stay had been a big mistake. But he couldn't renege now.

A deal was a deal.

"Don't try to pull the wool over my eyes." Mrs. Stokes said. "Foreclosing on the Holiday Ranch wasn't just business and you and I both know it. I had a front-row seat to your infatuation with Liberty Holiday and witnessed with my own two eyes how hurt you were after your date with her."

Mrs. Stokes was one of the few people Corbin had told about the twin switch. Sunny and Jesse were the other two. His siblings hadn't thought it was that big a deal. Mrs. Stokes was more sympathetic.

"And I understand why. No one likes being duped."

Corbin had been duped. Until the date, his infatuation with Liberty had been all about her looks and popularity. During the date, he'd started seeing the real person behind the beautiful homecoming queen façade. A sweet person who seemed to care about his thoughts and feelings.

And maybe that's what had hurt the most.

Belle hadn't cared. She'd just been following her sister's orders.

Mrs. Stokes coughing pulled him from his thoughts. She'd always had a smoker's cough, but now it sounded much worse. As soon as she stopped coughing, he voiced his concern.

"You need to stop smoking. It's going to kill you."

She shrugged. "If not it, something else."

"Then let it be something else."

She studied him. "You love to act like you don't care about anything or anyone, but you care, Corbin Whitlock. You care a lot."

"Nope, I'm more of the town villain."

She grinned. "Maybe that's why I like you so much. I've always had a thing for bad boys."

"I doubt a podiatrist is much of a bad boy."

"You heard about that, did ya? Well, Jeffrey isn't my boyfriend anymore. He gave great foot massages, but was boring as hell. He knew absolutely nothing about business. Which leaves me dateless for the Memorial Day picnic this weekend." Her eyes narrowed. "Unless the town villain would like to escort me and entertain me with how he made his millions?"

He couldn't help laughing at the woman's audacity. "I'll be happy to escort you, but only if you promise not to smoke. You might not care about your lungs, but I care about mine."

She snorted. "Prissy."

After Corbin left the bank, he headed back to the ranch. Hank was going to show him how to clean Homer's hoofs—something he wasn't looking forward to. But on his way out of town, he passed a car sitting on the opposite side of the road. He cussed when he recognized the face of the woman behind the wheel. From that distance, he wasn't sure which twin it was, but it didn't matter. He couldn't ignore a stranded woman.

Even a Holiday.

He made a U-turn and pulled in behind her, then got out and walked to the driver's side. She was staring out the windshield and didn't see him until he was standing at the window. She startled and turned to him.

He recognized Belle immediately. She was crying, and looking into her watery green eyes made him feel like he'd swallowed a grapefruit whole. She quickly looked away and swiped at her eyes before she rolled down the window.

"Hey." Her voice sounded nasally and unsteady. "I was just . . . taking a phone call and didn't want to drive and talk."

Her cellphone was nowhere in sight, but he went along with the lie. "Smart."

"And my allergies are kicking up." She grabbed a tissue out of her purse and he noticed her hand shaking.

"Allergies are bad this time of year." He sighed. "Look. Are you okay?"

She pinned on a fake smile. "I'm fine. Perfectly fine."

"You sure? I can give you a ride back to the Remingtons' Ranch if you want. Rome can send someone to pick up your car later."

"No! I mean I'm not ready to go back yet. I just need . . ." She let the sentence trail off as if she didn't know how to finish it. So he finished it for her.

"A stiff drink?"

She blinked and a determined look settled over her features. "Yes. As a matter of fact that's exactly what I need. A stiff drink. Thank you." Without another word, she put the car into drive and pulled away, leaving him standing on the side of the road in confusion.

He figured he had two choices. He could get back in his truck and mind his own damn business. Or he could follow her and make sure she didn't take his advice and get into trouble. If she was going where he thought she was going, she could easily get into trouble.

The Hellhole was a family restaurant that served the best barbecue in the county . . . or some said the entire world. It was also a cowboy bar that could get real rowdy later in the night. Luckily, it was still early when Corbin stepped in the door. The spicy scent of smoking meat made his stomach rumble. No one made barbecue like Bobby Jay. But since taking over the Holiday Ranch, Corbin had stayed away from the bar. If the glares he was receiving were any indication, it had been a smart choice.

Too bad Belle had taken that choice from him.

He found her sitting at one end of the bar. He could have taken a seat at a table and kept an eye on her from a distance, but he had never been a covert kind of guy. He took the stool next to her, wincing when his butt hit the hard wood.

She turned to him with surprise. "What are you doing?"

He took off his hat and set it on the bar. "I needed a stiff drink too." He motioned for the bartender and ordered baby back ribs and whiskey, then looked at Belle. "And the lady will have . . ."

"The same."

He squinted at her. "You sure you wouldn't like something else to drink?"

She lifted her chin. "Are you saying I don't know my own mind?"

He looked back at the bartender. "Whiskey it is." After he left to fill their order, Corbin glanced at Belle. She was dressed in business attire—caramel-colored wide-legged pants and an off-white button-up shirt—like she had just come from work. Since she had been sitting on the road just outside Mrs. Fields' property, he figured that was the case. "Jesse told me about you moving your office from Houston to the carriage house. He keeps asking me to stop by and see the renovations he's done, but I haven't had the time." Plus, he didn't want to run into the twins.

And yet, here he was.

"And you must see the renovations your brother did." Her tone was dramatic and snide. "I'm sure you'll lo-o-ove them as much as my sister does." Their drinks arrived and she didn't hesitate to take a big swig ... and then choked as if she'd just scorched her throat with a torch.

"Easy there." He patted her back until she caught her breath. "You sure you don't want something a little weaker?"

Green daggers shot from her eyes. "Because I'm the weaker twin—the twin who can't handle strong liquor or make my own decisions. I need to stick with elderberry wine and letting everyone else tell me what's right for me." She jabbed a finger at him. "Well, let me tell you something, Corbin Whitlock, I can handle whiskey and my own damn life!" She kept eye contact with him as she picked up her glass and downed the rest of the whiskey in one gulp. Her eyes watered and a shiver ran through her body, but she didn't choke this time. After a deep, quivery breath, she held up her empty glass and yelled at the bartender. "Another, please!" Corbin opened his mouth, but closed it again when she shot him a warning look. "Don't you dare say a word."

He held up his hands. "My lips are sealed. But just for the record, I never thought of you as the weaker twin."

She snorted. "Ha! Go lie to someone else. Everyone in town thinks I'm the weaker twin."

"I don't think that's true. Yes, Liberty is the most outspoken between the two of you. She's certainly more controlling. But that doesn't mean she's the strongest and you're the weakest. Take me and Sunny, for example. Some people might look at us and say I'm the strongest because I'm more controlling. They might think I tell Sunny what to do and when to do it. The truth is that Sunny has a mind of her own. If she wants something, she usually gets it—whether I like her choice or not."

He must have said the wrong thing because tears filled her eyes.

"But that's the problem," she said. "I don't have a mind of my own. All my life, Liberty has made most of my decisions for me. Sadly, I wanted her to. I trust her decisions much more than I trust my own." A tear rolled down her cheek and that grapefruit-sized knot returned to his throat. "Now, I realize that she's not always going to be there to make those decisions . . . and that's why I'm sitting here feeling totally and completely lost." Her drink arrived and half of it was gone before he could blink.

He really didn't want to get involved in Belle Holiday's problems. But if he didn't, he was afraid she was going to die from alcohol poisoning. He picked up a cocktail napkin and held it out. When she was too lost in her misery to notice it, he took her chin and turned her to face him.

"You aren't lost." He gently blotted the tears from her cheeks. "You're just feeling that way because things are changing. Nobody likes change. It makes them feel uncomfortable and out of control."

She sniffed. "I bet you've never felt lost or out of control. You're like Liberty. Nothing shakes y'all."

"Things shake us. We're just better at hiding it."

"What shakes you?"

At the moment, it was the mismatched teary green eyes that were staring back at him from only inches away. They held him captive and he couldn't look away. Nor could he stop the truth from spilling out.

"Sunny being hurt or unhappy shakes me. And every time my mama dropped me and Sunny off with another relative. That shook me up real bad. Which was stupid. It happened so often you would have thought I'd have expected it. But nope. Every time she and Daddy came and got us, I thought they had fixed all the problems in their marriage and we would live as a happy family forever. A few months later, they'd start fighting and we'd be dropped off again. It wasn't until she left us with Uncle Dan that the truth finally hit me . . . we weren't a happy family and never would be."

Two tears spilled from her eyes and trickled down her cheeks. This time, the knot that formed in his throat felt like a boulder.

Because this time, he knew the tears were for him.

Chapter Eight

Belle felt like a complete fool.

"I'm so sorry," she said. "I'm sitting here whining about my own problems when your life was so . . ." She wanted to say heartbreaking, but she knew he wasn't the type of man who would want sympathy so she chose another word. "Hard."

He handed her the cocktail napkin. "You don't need to be sorry. Sunny and I survived and are doing just fine . . . when she's not driving me to drink with her dangerous exploits."

"What kind of dangerous exploits?"

"Skydiving, race car driving . . . horseback riding. If it scares the hell out me, Sunny wants to do it."

"Maybe she's not trying to scare you. Maybe she's just trying to be her own woman."

"Doing dangerous things doesn't make you your own woman, Belle." He glanced down at the glass of whiskey. "Neither does drinking whiskey. Do you even like whiskey?"

She really wanted to lie, but the knowing look in his eyes stopped her. "It's nasty stuff."

He smiled. He had a really nice smile. It was the kind that totally transformed his face from handsome to breath stealing. "Okay. We've figured a couple things out. You don't like licorice ice cream and whiskey. What drink would you like?"

"Liberty always orders us—"

He cut her off. "We're not talking about what Liberty always orders for you. What do you want?"

"That's the problem. I've let Liberty take control for so long that I don't have a clue."

"Then let's figure it out." He waved over the bartender. "The lady would like one each of your most popular cocktails, please."

"What are you doing?" she asked once the bartender was gone. "That's a horrible waste of money."

He winked. "Luckily, I have money to waste."

The bartender only brought two drinks at a time, but she had to take sips of seven different cocktails until she found the one she liked the best. As soon as she took a sip, she knew. Corbin seemed to know too.

"If that look of utter delight is any indication, I think we have a winner. You're a lemon drop martini girl."

She took another sip. "It tastes like summer. It's refreshing like a dip in Cooper Springs and sweetly tart like Mama's lemonade. And it gives you a warm feeling right here." She pressed a hand to her chest. Corbin's gaze followed and that warm feeling intensified.

"I think that warm feeling has more to do with

all the alcohol you've consumed." His gaze lifted, his eyes a dark blue that beckoned her to dive in and swim around. The crazy thought had her realizing that she probably was a little tipsy. She looked away and continued eating the baby back ribs, potato salad, and beans the bartender had brought.

She'd forgotten how good Bobby Jay's ribs were. She usually ordered the brisket like Liberty, but now she realized she loved ribs much better. Although she didn't like them as much as Corbin. He finished off his plate and then started helping himself to some of hers.

"Hey, rib stealing is a crime here in Wilder," she teased.

"I figured you wouldn't mind sharing with the man who helped you find lemon drop martinis." He took a big bite from the rib he held.

When they had finished polishing off the ribs, he asked for the tab and refused to accept the credit card she tried to hand him. "My treat and I'll drive you back to the Remington Ranch. You can come get your car tomorrow."

He was right. She was too tipsy to drive. But she didn't want to go back to her sister's.

"I don't want to go to the Remington Ranch."

He cocked his head in confusion and a strand of hair fell over his forehead. It reminded her of the wayward mop of hair he'd had in high school. Unruly and unstyled. He had gorgeous wavy dark blond hair with brown undertones. On their date, she had wanted to reach out and run her fingers through the silky-looking strands.

Of course, she had been too shy and terrified of being found out then.

She wasn't now.

Without hesitation, she reached out and tousled his hair, causing more than one strand to fall over his forehead in messy waves.

His shocked look made her realize how inappropriate her actions were. But she wasn't sorry. She liked messy-haired, casual Corbin much more than she liked styled, rigid businessman Corbin.

She lowered her hand from his hair and smiled. "There's the boy I remember."

His features hardened. "I'll never be that foolish boy again."

"You weren't foolish, Corbin. You just liked a girl, that's all."

"And foolishly pursued her with wilted wildflowers and silly poems as if I would have ever stood a chance."

"That's what I admired most about you. There were a lot of boys who fell under Liberty's spell, but most of them didn't have the guts to do what you did and go for it. I don't think that's foolish. I think that's brave. I, on the other hand, wasn't brave. I wasn't brave enough to tell my sister I wasn't going to lie for her. Or brave enough to tell you the truth. And I'm not brave enough now either. I'm shaking in my boots just thinking about having to live on my own and make my own decisions. But it looks like I don't get a choice."

He studied her. "Sometimes not having a

choice is exactly what makes us brave." He got up. "Now come on, I'll drive you home."

She shook her head. "No. I mean it. I'm not going back to Cloe's. She doesn't need me staying in the room she should be decorating for her and Rome's baby."

"Then I'll take you to Sweetie's."

"Sweetie and Decker don't need me butting into their lives either."

He studied her for a long moment before he sighed. "Fine. There's room at the ranch. You can stay there until you figure out what you want to do."

She was more than a little surprised. "You'd let me stay at the ranch after what I did to you?"

"I'm already stuck with three Holidays. What's one more?" He grabbed his hat and tugged it on.

She should have taken him up on the offer, but she couldn't. "Thank you. But if I'm going to learn to stand on my own two feet, I need to start now. I can drive myself to a hotel." She stood and the floor shifted beneath her feet.

"Like hell you can." He hooked an arm around her waist to steady her, except the feel of his strong fingers curling over her hip made her feel anything but steady. "Nor am I dropping you off at some seedy hotel and those are the only ones remotely close to Wilder."

She frowned at him. "The last thing I want right now is someone else telling me what I should do."

"I get it, and if you hadn't imbibed too much

alcohol tonight, I would be more than happy to let you go wherever you wanted to go. But since I contributed to your drinking, I can't do that."

He was right, but she still couldn't concede. "I don't want to be around family right now. I need some space to figure things out."

A long moment passed before he spoke. "I have another option. It's not The Ritz Carlton, but it will give you the space you seem to think you need."

The beat-up trailer he drove her to was about as far from The Ritz as you could get. "Whose is this?" she asked when he pulled his big truck into the dirt lot.

"It's mine. It used to be my Uncle Dan's."

Belle had known Dan Wheeler lived in a trailer. She just hadn't realized its condition. As she took in the broken windows and rusted siding, her heart ached for Dan . . . and the two teenagers who'd had to live here with him.

Corbin shut off the engine and turned to her. "You can still come back to the ranch with me. I'm sure your family would be thrilled."

"But you wouldn't." When he didn't reply, she shook her head. "No. This is good."

"Suit yourself."

The inside of the trailer wasn't much better than the outside.

"It's very . . . nice," she lied.

He laughed. "There are clean sheets in the hall linen cabinet and there's a new toothbrush and some toothpaste in the top drawer in the bathroom. Lock the door when I leave and call if there are any problems. Do you need me to come pick you up in the morning to get your car?"

"Thank you, but you've done enough. Especially after what I did to you. I'm sorry, Corbin. I'm truly sorry."

He nodded. "How about if we let that night go?"

"Can you?"

He hesitated and his gaze lowered to her mouth. She had thought she'd sobered up on the drive to the trailer, but if the warm feeling in her tummy and the dizzy feeling in her head were any indication, she wasn't sober. When Corbin took a step closer, her lips parted on a soft exhalation as her eyes slid closed. But instead of feeling the soft press of his kiss, he spoke.

"Good night."

When she opened her eyes, he was already heading out the door. Once he was gone, she felt like a complete fool. Corbin wasn't going to kiss her. He had never been interested it her.

It was Liberty.

Always Liberty.

She locked the door and glanced around the trailer. She had spent the last couple months living alone while Liberty had been helping to untangle things at the ranch. She hadn't liked coming home every night to an empty apartment, but that loneliness had felt nothing like this loneliness. Probably because she'd known it was only temporary. Liberty would come back and they'd live like two peas in a pod once again.

But Liberty had found another pea and another

pod, leaving Belle with only two choices. She could try to squeeze into one of her sisters' or her parents' pods. Or she could put on her big-girl panties and get used to being a single pea.

Moving in with one of her sisters would be safe, but maybe it was time to stop playing it safe. Maybe it was time to start making her own decisions—even if they turned out to be the wrong ones.

Tonight, she had tasted a lot of drinks before she'd gotten to the lemon drop martini. Once she'd taken the first sip, she'd known it was the drink for her. Maybe that's what she needed to do in life. She just needed to keep trying things until she discovered what she liked and what she wanted.

She didn't know why an image of Corbin popped into her head at that exact moment. But there he was, his wavy hair all tousled from her fingers and his blue eyes filled with surprise that she had touched him. There was something about his surprise that had made her feel powerful. Probably because she rarely surprised people. She was the compliant twin who went along with everyone.

It was time for that to change.

She fired off a text message to Cloe telling her that she wouldn't be home. She lied and said she was staying at Sweetie's. If she'd told the truth, Cloe would be over in a New York second to find out what was going on. It would be better if Belle explained everything in the morning.

There were two bedrooms in the trailer. One

had a bed and one had a mattress on the floor. Since the one with the bed had a floral bedspread, she assumed it was Sunny's and chose it. Corbin had already screwed with her head enough tonight. She didn't need to sleep on a pillow that smelled like him.

She slept much better than she thought she would in a strange place. She woke up the next morning with a slight hangover and the sun shining brightly in the window. She reached for her cellphone on the nightstand to see what time it was, but since she hadn't charged it, it was dead. She went to set it back on the nightstand and noticed the sketchpad.

Everyone at school had known Sunny loved to draw. She'd taken a sketchpad with her everywhere. Belle couldn't help picking it up and taking a peek inside. As soon as she opened the sketchpad, she realized Sunny wasn't just a doodler. She was an artist.

Her drawings brought her subjects to life. There were drawings of the townsfolk—Mrs. Stokes in her ratty mink, Sheryl Ann baking in her kitchen, Mr. Crawley standing behind the counter of the general store. There were drawings of animals—a sad-looking mutt dog sitting by a dumpster, a long-horned cow munching grass, a litter of kittens snuggled in a cardboard box labeled FREE.

There was a drawing of a teenage Corbin sitting on his old bike in front of the trailer. He wore a stretched out T-shirt and frayed cut-off jean shorts. His tube socks drooped around his tattered running shoes and the bill of his ball cap sat crooked on his mop of hair. He was laughing. Belle couldn't remember ever seeing him laugh like that with his mouth open and his eyes crinkled at the corners. Just looking at it made her smile.

The smile faded when she came to the next few drawings.

They were all of the Holiday Ranch. Every detail was right, from the swing in the old oak to the peonies in Mimi's garden. In one, Sunny had even put their old barn cat, Mouser, peeking out of the barn. In another, a much younger Mimi was working in her garden. In another, teenage Belle and her sisters were all squeezed together on the porch swing, laughing.

Belle now knew why Corbin had wanted to give the ranch to his sister. Sunny's infatuation with it was there in every pencil stroke.

A banging on the front door had Belle jumping. She quickly closed the sketchpad and put it back on the nightstand before she hurried to the door. When she pulled it open, she found Sweetie, Cloe, and Liberty standing there.

They did not look happy.

"What the hell, Belle!" Liberty hollered.

"There's no need to yell at her, Libby," Cloe said. "She looks like she's had a rough night."

Liberty glared at her. "And I'm about to give her a rough morning."

Sweetie's expression was less hostile and more concerned. "What were you thinking, Belly? We've been worried sick since Cloe called me this morning. Why would you say you were staying with me when you weren't? And why didn't you answer your phone? Thankfully, when we called the ranch to see if you were there Corbin knew where you were."

"I'm sorry," Belle said. "I just knew you'd want to come check on me and I needed some time to think."

"To think!" Liberty yelled.

Sweetie held up a hand. "Simmer down, Libby. How about we all go to Nothin' But Muffins and talk calmly? I'm starving."

Nothin' But Muffins was the spot to be in the mornings. The small coffee shop was filled to the rafters when they stepped in the door. Everyone greeted them with big smiles and a hearty "Good mornin'!" as they stood in line to place their orders with the owner, Sheryl Ann.

Belle couldn't decide what muffin she wanted to go with her herbal tea so she ordered a half dozen different ones. Since there were no tables inside, she and her sisters moved outside to the picnic tables. When she opened her box of muffins and started taking bites of each one, her sisters stared at her with surprise.

"What's wrong?" she asked around a mouthful of a Sour Lemon Poppy muffin.

"We thought you'd ordered for all of us," Sweetie said.

She swallowed the bite of muffin. "Oh. Sorry." She handed the lemon poppyseed muffin to Sweetie. "But I'm happy to share the ones I don't like."

Liberty stared at her. "You've lost it, Belly.

Really lost it. I get you're upset that I'm marrying Jesse, but you need to get over it."

"I'm over it." She tasted Pea-Nutty Buddy and her eyes widened. "This is it! This is the best muffin ever."

"What about Cocoa Java Junkie? I thought that was your favorite."

Belle picked up the Cocoa Java Junkie muffin and set it in front of Liberty. "It's your favorite. It has always had too much coffee flavor for me."

Liberty studied her, and as always, read her well. "So you want to make your own decisions. Is that it? Well, that's great. It's about time. We have an entire calendar of events we need to do, both here and in Houston, and I can't be two places at once. So you'll have to do the events in Houston and I'll do the ones here."

Normally, Belle would agree. But she wasn't in an agreeable mood today. "No."

Liberty huffed. "Fine. You do the ones here and I'll do the ones in Houston."

Belle took another bite of muffin before she spoke. "You misunderstood me. I'm not doing either. I'm taking some time off."

She didn't know who was more surprised by her words, she or Liberty. Probably Liberty. Her eyes were wide and her mouth gaped open. Belle could tell by the tic at the corner of her eye that things were about to get ugly. Sweetie and Cloe knew it too. They both rested their hands on Liberty's arms as if to keep her seated.

"Now, Libby," Sweetie said. "There's no need to get upset. I'm sure Belle has a good reason for needing some time off." She looked at Belle, who finished off her muffin and wiped her mouth with a napkin before she spoke.

"Not really. And it's not like it's surprising. I was planning to take some time off anyway to help Mama and Daddy sell the ranch—"

Liberty cut her off. "Mama and Daddy aren't selling the ranch anymore. It's not theirs to sell!"

"I know that. But we still planned for me to take off this month. Which is why we didn't take on as many events as we normally do. It was you who added more to our calendar by agreeing to do events for the townsfolk—without even consulting me, I might add." She shrugged. "So it's you who needs to figure out how to take care of those events." She got up. "Now if you'll excuse me, I need to order another Pea-Nutty Buddy. Who knew I was such a peanut butter fan?"

Chapter Nine

"DON'T LOOK SO grumpy, Cory." Sunny shot him a bright smile. "This is fun!"

This wasn't even close to what Corbin would consider fun. He'd planned on letting his sore butt heal before he got back on a horse. All it had taken was one of Sunny's puppy dog looks to have him bouncing along on the back of Homer with his teeth jarring and his still-sore butt aching.

He was a complete sucker.

And not just for Sunny.

Mimi bossed him around like he was a wet-behind-the-ears kid. Just this morning, she had gotten after him for holding Tay too much. So now the kitten was wandering around the ranch and getting into things she had no business getting into.

Then there was Darla Holiday. The woman had completely won him over with her baking. She had figured out he had a sweet tooth and was constantly bringing him cookies, brownies, and pies he couldn't resist.

The only one who hadn't turned him into

putty in their hands was Hank. But with the way the older man had taken Sunny under his wing, Corbin didn't dislike him as much as he used to.

Then there was Belle. What had he been thinking to offer her his trailer? But it had been impossible not to when she had looked like a little lost lamb that couldn't find its way back to the flock.

Except she wasn't a little lost lamb. She was a full-grown woman. A woman who had kept him up for the last two nights with thoughts of her sleeping in his trailer. Had she slept in his bed? Had she rested that mane of ebony curls on his pillow? Tucked those long legs under his sheets? Had she showered in the tiny shower? Lathered her hands with his soap and run them over her curvy hips and perfect breasts?

And if those thoughts weren't bad enough, he couldn't stop thinking about the kisses they'd shared on their date.

Belle might be the tentative twin, but she wasn't a tentative kisser. On the front porch, she'd kissed him with hot slides of her lips and demanding thrusts of her tongue until he had been so hard he'd worried about climaxing in his jeans. The other night, he'd wanted to feel those lips again. When she'd released that breathy little sigh and closed her eyes, he'd been seconds from giving into the temptation.

Thankfully, he came to his senses and left.

Now he just wished he could get her to leave his mind.

"Did you hear about Jesse and Liberty going to Houston?" Sunny cut into his thoughts.

He adjusted his butt in the saddle. "No. What are they doing in Houston?"

"I guess Liberty has some events there this weekend and needs Jesse to help her."

"Why isn't Belle helping her?"

"According to Jesse, Belle decided to take some time off. Now Liberty is stuck doing all the events on her own. She's having Cloe and Sweetie help her with the Memorial Day picnic this weekend, while she and Jesse are in Houston doing a wedding and anniversary." She laughed. "I can't shake the image of our rodeo cowboy big brother fluffing a bride's veil before she walks down the aisle."

Corbin didn't laugh. He was too focused on Belle suddenly taking time off from work. He knew she'd been upset the other night. Any fool could have seen that. But he figured she'd be over it by now and she and Liberty would have worked things out.

Obviously not.

"Is Belle okay?" he asked.

"Jesse doesn't think so. I guess she moved out of Cloe's house and is staying in some hotel."

"And they let her?"

Sunny glanced over at him. "She's an adult woman, Cory. She gets to make the choice where she wants to live." Her eyes narrowed. "And why are you worried about Belle, anyway? I thought you didn't like her."

It was a good question. He wished he had

a good answer. Before he could make one up, Sunny glanced over his shoulder and her eyes widened. "Oh, no!" Without any warning, she urged her horse into a gallop.

Homer, being the follower that he was, took off after her, with Corbin hanging on for dear life and praying he wouldn't fall off and break his neck. Once Homer slowed, Corbin saw what had caused Sunny's concern. A longhorn steer had gotten stuck in an overgrown mesquite tree. Sunny never could ignore an animal in distress. As soon as she reached the tree, she jumped off her horse. Which scared Corbin to death.

"No, Sunny!" he yelled as he dismounted and pulled out his phone. "I'll call Hank."

"We can't wait for Hank. Look how scared he is."

He didn't look scared to Corbin. He looked pissed off. The animal was twisting his head back and forth, his sharp horns poking out of the branches like twin daggers.

"I mean it, Sunny," Corbin said. "Get back on your horse. I'll handle this."

"You don't know anything about cattle."

"Neither do you. Now get back on your horse. I'll free him. Please, Sunny." Please was the one word that worked the best with his sister. Probably because he only used it when he was about to have a heart attack.

"Fine. But don't you dare get gored. You might be an annoying big brother, but I've gotten used to you."

Once Sunny was safely on her horse, Corbin

tied Homer's reins to a mesquite branch and moved closer to the struggling steer. "Easy there, big fella. I'm here to help." The animal rolled his eyes at him and continued to tug at his extremely sharp-looking horns entangled in the gnarled branches of the tree. "Bring me your rope, Sunny."

Sunny moved her horse up next to him and handed him her rope. It took some doing to get the rope tied around the thick branch that was holding the steer. Especially when trying to avoid thrashing horns. Once Corbin felt like it was secure enough, he tossed the other end to Sunny.

"Wrap that around your saddle horn and see if you can break that branch off."

She nodded and wrapped the rope around the saddle horn before she clicked her tongue and the horse started backing up. It didn't take much to break off the branch and free the steer. Corbin got ready to jump out of the way in case the cow charged. But the steer merely shook his head and then continued eating the grass beneath the tree as if he hadn't just gotten stuck in it.

"We did it!" Sunny crowed. "We're ranchers!"

"More like two greenhorns who just got lucky," he said, but Corbin couldn't help grinning the entire ride home. When they got back to the ranch, Hank stepped out of the barn to help Sunny dismount and she couldn't wait to tell him all about their rescue.

"You should have seen him, Hank. Cory didn't even blink. He just walked straight toward that big bull and freed him."

"It wasn't a bull, Sunny," Corbin corrected. "It

was a steer." Hank looked at him with surprise and Corbin couldn't help wondering if he'd made a mistake. "A steer has been castrated, right?"

Hank studied him intently. "That's right. And you got that steer out?"

"Yes, sir." The sir just popped out. Annoyed, he added, "It's my steer, after all." He started unsaddling Homer. A thump on the back startled him and he glanced up to see Hank standing there.

"Good job."

Once Corbin finished unsaddling Homer and made sure he was groomed and had water, he headed to the house to get some work done. The Wi-Fi company had sent a guy out the day before so Corbin had a lot of catching up to do. But once in his office with Tay cuddled on his lap, he couldn't seem to stay focused. His mind kept wandering to Belle being all alone in a dreary hotel room.

After trying to read through a contract for the sixth time without retaining any of the words, he finally gave up and went in search of Mimi. He found her out front in her flower garden.

"Sounds like you had an exciting afternoon," she said as soon as she glanced up and saw him standing on the porch. Tay wiggled to get down. When he set her on the porch, she leapt down the steps and weaved her way through the flowers to greet the old woman. Mimi laughed and took off one gardening glove to pet the kitten.

Corbin sat down on the top step. "Sunny exaggerates my abilities."

Mimi shot him a glance from under the wide

brim of her hat. "I doubt that. You seem pretty capable, Cory. And it wasn't Sunny who told me. It was Hank."

Again, he felt annoyed. He'd done nothing to endear himself to the Holidays. In fact, he'd done just the opposite. So why were they being so nice to him? No doubt, they were only sucking up so he'd allow them to stay longer. Well, it wasn't happening. When the month was up, they were gone. So they didn't need to waste their hospitality on him.

Especially when there was someone in their family who needed it more.

"Belle is pretty upset about Jesse and Liberty getting married," he said.

Mimi didn't look surprised by the sudden change of subject. She tugged on her glove and went back to pulling weeds. "I think that was pretty apparent the other night when they made the announcement. And it makes sense. Belle and Liberty aren't just sisters. They're twins. They've spent their entire lives sharing everything. Marriage is something they can't share. It has to be hard for Belle."

"I think that's putting it mildly. I guess you've heard about her taking time off from her business."

"I heard." She chuckled. "Liberty is fit to be tied."

Her amusement surprised him. "You think it's funny? Because the emotional state your granddaughter was in the other night wasn't funny."

Mimi stopped weeding and looked at him.

"I heard about you helping out Belle by offering her your trailer to stay in. Seems you keep coming to her rescue. Are you interested in my granddaughter, Cory?"

His annoyance shot to anger. "Not hardly. At least not in the way you're intimating. But I'm not going to ignore someone who is going through a tough time like you and your family seem to be doing. Belle obviously needs your support right now and you're here weeding your garden, Miss Darla is inside baking cookies, Hank is doing Lord knows what, and Liberty's off in Houston. No one seems to give a damn about Belle being alone in some seedy hotel."

He thought Mimi would be offended by his outburst, but if her smile was any indication, she was delighted. "It certainly seems like you give a damn. And you're wrong. I do care about Belle being upset and so does the rest of the family."

"Then why haven't you talked her into staying with one of her sisters . . . or here?"

Her eyes widened. "You'd allow her to stay here?"

"Since the place is already overrun with Holidays, one more wouldn't make a difference." He pointed a finger at her. "But only until the end of June. No Holiday is staying longer than that."

She smiled. "Of course not. Unfortunately, I don't think Belle would agree to that. Nor does she want to stay with her sisters. And I get it. She needs time to figure out who she is and what she wants. She needs to learn how to stand on her own two feet."

"I don't doubt Belle needs some space to figure out who she is, but she also needs support." He knew from experience that life lessons were brutal and if you didn't have someone to love and support you, it was hard to get through the bad times. He didn't know what he would have done without Sunny.

"I agree. But there's a difference between support and smothering." She nodded at Tay, who was lying on her back batting at a drooping flower. "Take that kitten for example. If you don't let her get used to the ranch and figure out how to avoid the dangers, she'll never learn. There will come a point when she doesn't want to. She'll just sit in her cat contraption all day staring out the window and not realizing how much fun she could be having." She hesitated. "The same goes for Sunny."

"Believe me, Sunny will never miss out on having fun."

Mimi laughed. "True, but she relies on you more than you think. And while it's good to have a safety net to fall back on, you also need to learn how to rely on yourself. That's what Belle is learning now. She's learning to trust herself and her decisions. The last thing she needs is another family member coming to her rescue and making decisions for her." She sent him a pointed look. "But a friend's support wouldn't be a bad thing."

It took him a moment to figure out what she was saying. He held up his hands. "Oh, no. Belle and I aren't friends. Far from it."

"Really? Because you being worried about

her says differently." Before he could continue to argue the point, she glanced at her flowers. "Would you look at my poor babies?" She lifted the bloom Tay had been swatting at and shook her head. "They're getting all wilted in this heat." She glanced at Corbin. "Could you do me a big favor? I'm all out of fertilizer. Could you pick some up for me at the hardware store? It doesn't have to be right now. Just whenever you go to town." She sent him a pleading look. "Although the sooner the better."

Corbin hadn't planned on going into town. He had work to do. He glanced at the sun edging lower in the sky. Although it looked like he'd already wasted most of the day. He might as well start fresh tomorrow morning.

"Fine. I'll go into town." He got to his feet and went to pick up Tay, but then he remembered Mimi's words and stopped. "I guess Tay can stay here—but if anything happens to her, it's on you."

Mimi smiled. "I'll guard her with my life." She went back to weeding. "And while you're in town, you might want to stop by your trailer. Belle is a sweetheart, but she's always been a little absentminded. I wouldn't be surprised if she forgot to lock up."

Belle had never acted absentminded to him, but Corbin figured Mimi knew her granddaughter better than he did. Besides, he had left one of his favorite western shirts at the trailer and needed to pick it up.

But before he stopped off at the hardware store and his trailer, he drove an extra twenty minutes out of town to the closest hotel. He knew he had no business doing it, but damned if he could stop himself. Nor could he stop himself from being worried when the front desk guy informed him that Belle wasn't registered there.

He called three other hotels in the vicinity and she wasn't at any of them. Which made him wonder if maybe she'd decided to stay with one of her sisters, after all. Since he certainly wasn't about to call every Holiday sister to find out, he decided to let it go.

Belle Holiday wasn't his concern.

At least that's what he tried to tell himself. But if that were the case, then why was he flooded with relief when he got to his trailer and discovered her car sitting in front?

He got out of his truck and headed inside expecting to find Belle looking as sad and lost as she had the other night. But that wasn't what he found. Instead, he found her sprawled out on the couch wearing his favorite western shirt surrounded by a pile of snacks and looking as happy as a pig in mud. Her smile brightened when she saw him and she held up the bag in her hand.

"Hey, Corbin! Flamin' Cheeto?"

Chapter Ten

WHEN CORBIN ONLY stood there staring, Belle quickly sat up and tried to explain.

"I bet you're probably wondering what I'm still doing here. You see I was planning on getting a hotel room last night. But you're right. The hotels anywhere close to town are a little seedy. And I just can't stay with my family right now. So I thought you wouldn't mind if I stayed a couple nights until I figured out what I wanted to do. But if you're not agreeable to that, I'll—" She cut off when Corbin held up a hand and stopped her.

Usually, he was dressed to perfection—his hair styled back, his T-shirts and western shirts spotless and wrinkle-free, and his boots polished. Today, his T-shirt was streaked with dirt and there was a tear in his jeans and mud on his boots. When he pulled off his hat and tossed it to the kitchen table, his hair looked sweaty and mussed.

Why this dirty, sweaty Corbin caused a tingle of sexual awareness to settle in the pit of her stomach, Belle didn't know. But there it was, making her feel more than a little confused.

Corbin studied her for a long, tummy-tingling moment before he glanced down at the chips, candy, and soda cans that filled the coffee table. "Did you buy out Crawley's entire snack section?"

She blushed. "I guess it looks like it, doesn't it? And it's all your fault. I had so much fun trying all the different drinks at the Hellhole, I decided to do the same with snacks."

He arched an eyebrow. "And what conclusion did you come to?"

"Flamin' Hot Cheetos are now my favorite chip. Chocolate Frosted Donut KitKats my favorite candy and Wild Cherry Pepsi my favorite soda."

"I have to disagree." He picked up the bag of barbecue chips and ate a chip. "Kettle Backyard Barbeque chips beat out Flamin' Cheetos any day and no soda on God's green earth will ever beat out Dr Pepper."

She laughed. "Spoken like a true Texan. And what about candy?"

"I like it all." He sat down on the couch next to her and picked up the KitKats and snapped off a bar. He finished the entire thing in two bites. "Damn. You're right. These are good." He glanced at the television where a commercial was playing. "So what are you watching?"

"Hope Floats." When he didn't appear happy with her choice, she amended. "But we could watch something else if you want."

He shook his head. "Your decision, remember?"

"But it's your home."

He toed off his boots and placed his feet on the coffee table. "Not anymore."

It should have been awkward watching a movie with a man she wasn't sure even liked her. But for some reason, it wasn't. Probably because this relaxed Corbin was different than the inflexible Corbin. She was surprised to see he had a hole in one sock and the tip of his big toe stuck out. It was somehow sweet and endearing. As were the flecks of barbecue dust on the corner of his mouth and the way he tried all the different candy she'd bought.

He was eating a Red Vines licorice when he glanced over and caught her staring at him. "What?"

"Nothing. I just noticed that you're a little ... mussed. Did Daddy have you working on the ranch today?"

Both eyebrows lifted. "I don't work for your daddy."

"I didn't mean that. You just look like you've been doing manual labor."

He glanced down at his shirt and brushed at a dirt spot. "Sunny and I ran across a steer caught in a mesquite tree and had to get him out. By Sunny's reaction when the steer was free, you would have thought we'd lassoed the moon."

Belle now understood why. "I saw her drawings of the ranch." When his gaze shot over to her, she blushed. "I know. I shouldn't have snooped, but now I get why you wanted her to have the ranch. It's obviously her dream."

He didn't answer right away. He just stared at

the television, his face set in its usual stern lines. But his voice wasn't stern when he spoke. It was soft and achingly sad.

"She did those drawings mostly from memory. Uncle Dan only took us to the Holiday Ranch a few times when he was working for your daddy. But it was like every detail was burned into her brain." He hesitated. "I get it. The Holiday Ranch is a picture-perfect home."

She knew she shouldn't side with Corbin. He was the man taking the ranch from her family. While she didn't agree with his methods, she now understood them. He wasn't a villain. He was just a man who loved his sister and wanted her to have the home she'd always dreamed about.

She reached out and touched his arm. "I understand. I would do just about anything for my sisters too."

He turned to her. "Then make up with Liberty and stop holing up here."

"I'm not holing up here." When he sent her a skeptical look, she sighed. "Okay, I'm holing up. But I just can't seem to think for myself when I'm around Liberty. It's my own fault. I've always just followed her lead. But now I need to figure out how to lead myself. And like Mimi says, I can't do that when Liberty and any of my sisters are around."

His eyes narrowed. "Mimi? You've talked with her?"

"She called me yesterday and again this morning to check on me. She's the one who talked me into taking a few days to figure things out . . . and the one who thought you wouldn't mind me staying here."

His eyes narrowed. "Of course she did."

"Something wrong?"

"Nothing's wrong. I'm just starting to realize how ma—smart your grandmother is." He glanced back at the television. "Are you that interested in this movie?"

"I've seen it about a hundred times. If you want to switch to something else, that's fine with me."

"Actually, I think I'd rather balance all this sugar with real food." He got up and held out a hand. "Come on. Let's go get some tacos."

Ever since Belle could remember Tito's Tacos truck had been parked in front of the town hall. The story went that Tito Senior had been relocating his family from El Paso to Dallas when his food truck had broken down in Wilder. Needing money for repairs, Tito had started making tacos and selling them to the townsfolk until he could get his truck fixed. But then other things started mysteriously happening to the truck—flat tires and missing engine parts. By the time all of those things got fixed, Tito and his family had gotten attached to Wilder and decided to stay.

Now Tito Junior ran the business and had added a variety of different tacos to the menu. Which, of course, made making a decision that much harder.

Belle studied the large chalk menu resting against the side of the truck. "I'm not sure if I want the fish tacos with mango salsa or the pulled pork with pico de gallo or the crispy chicken with spicy sour cream."

Corbin looked at TJ, who was waiting to take their order, and shrugged. "I guess we'll take two of each and a Dr Pepper and a Wild Cherry Pepsi."

They ate their taco feast at the tiny tables on the sidewalk in front of the truck. Strings of fairy lights draped from the top of the truck over the tables and reflected in Corbin's blue eyes like stars. Stars that Belle was having trouble looking away from.

"So?" he said once she'd tried each one of her tacos.

"Definitely, the fish tacos with mango salsa."

"Pulled pork all the way for me." He stole the rest of her pulled pork taco from the paper wrapper it rested on and finished it in two bites.

"Hey! Just because I like fish tacos better that didn't mean I didn't want the pulled pork too. It's definitely number two."

He shrugged as he finished chewing. "Why waste your time on second best?"

Since he had a good point, she couldn't argue. But she did steal the rest of his fish taco. When he stared at her with surprise, she laughed and ended up choking on a chunk of fish. He was still thumping her on the back when Melba Wadley spoke behind them.

"Well, isn't this a sweet scene right out of a romantic comedy? I didn't realize you two were dat—No, Mickey Gilley!"

While Corbin and Belle watched in stunned

horror, a big fuzzy dog pushed his way between them and devoured what was left of their tacos.

Melba grabbed the dog—that looked like a poodle mixed with Great Dane—by the collar and tugged him back from the table. "Now, Gilley, that's not the way to make a good first impression." The dog sat down on his haunches and licked his chops before sending Belle a sheepish grin that made her laugh.

"Well, hello, Gilley." She reached out to pet him, but Corbin stopped her.

"No, Bella!" Even her surprise at his sharply spoken words didn't stop the warmth his nickname always evoked. "Don't show any signs of liking that dog or he'll be yours. That's how I ended up with Taylor Swift."

He was right. Melba Wadley worked for Belle's brother-in-law, Sheriff Decker Carson, and a nicer woman you'd never meet. But when it came to finding homes for her foster animals, she was tenaciously stubborn. The last thing Belle needed was a huge dog . . . with the sweetest face she'd ever seen. Even covered in sour cream.

"Now what are you talking about, Corbin," Melba said. "You love Tay-Tay and Gilley will make a perfect companion for Belle. Especially since I heard she's disowned her family."

Belle stared at her. "Where in the world did you hear that? I didn't disown my family. I would never do that. I'm just . . . taking a break."

Melba looked confused. "A break from family? That just don't make sense. You're stuck with family . . . unless you have a falling-out." She eyeballed Corbin. "And I think I can figure out what the falling-out is about. You're dating the enemy."

Corbin didn't seem at all taken back, but Belle was.

"Firstly, Corbin and I are not dating. We're just . . ." She searched for a word to describe their relationship and came up empty. They weren't dating, but they certainly weren't friends either. She left the sentence hanging and moved on. "And secondly, he's not the enemy."

Melba looked thoroughly confused. "So he's not stealing your family's ranch?"

"He didn't steal anything. We defaulted on a loan and he just followed the contract my grandmother signed." Belle made the mistake of looking at the dog. He was giving her such a soulful look she couldn't help reaching out and stroking his fuzzy head. His eyes drifted closed as he snuggled against her palm.

Something that didn't go unnoticed by Melba.

"Would you look at that? Gilley looks like he's died and gone to doggie heaven. Of course, anything would be heaven after the hell this poor fella has been through. When I got him he was skinnier than a willow branch. Poor thing had been starved near to death."

Belle's heart tightened. "Starved?"

Corbin got up from the table. "As always, it was great seeing you, Melba, but we need to get going." He took Belle's arm and led her toward his truck.

Melba called after them. "If you change your

mind about needing a pet, Belle, you know where to find me!"

Belle glanced back over her shoulder to see Gilley sitting at Melba's feet looking forlorn.

"Don't look," Corbin said. "That's what suckered me in."

"Who starves an animal?"

He came to a stop and turned to her. "Do you want to go back? I just thought you had enough on your plate without worrying about a dog. But the choice is yours."

"You're right. I can't take care of a dog when I can't even take care of myself."

"That's not what I said." Corbin pulled open the passenger door of his truck. "I said you have a lot on your plate. I think you're taking pretty good care of yourself. You found a place to stay and are well fed. Or would have been if that huge hound hadn't finished it off."

Belle laughed and glanced back, but Melba and Gilley were already gone. Which made her sad.

Corbin sighed. "Like Melba said, you know where to find her if you change your mind."

She wouldn't. She didn't need a dog right now. But that didn't stop her from thinking about Gilley all the way back to the trailer.

Once there, Corbin hopped out and opened her door before he walked her to the foot of the rickety steps that led to the front door of the trailer.

"Well, thank you for dinner." To avoid another awkward moment like the other night, she quickly climbed the steps and pulled out the key so she could unlock the door. Unfortunately, she struggled to get the key in the lock.

Suddenly, Corbin was there, his muscle body and heat surrounding her as he took the key from her. Once the door was open, she held out her hand for the key, but rather than dropping it into her hand, he placed it carefully on her palm and closed her fingers around it. She knew he only did it so she wouldn't drop the key and they'd have to search for it in the dark. But the feel of his hand closed around hers sent a bolt of electricity arcing through her and her breath caught.

The sound seemed deafening in the silence of the night.

He stilled, a sure sign he'd heard. She should have pulled her hand away and made light of it. Instead, she just stood there with her pulse spiking and her insides sizzling and her gaze pinned on his perfect features that she could see in the flickering light of the television they'd left on.

"Was it a lie?" he said in a soft, husky voice that made her insides tremble. Her voice sounded just the opposite, high pitched and strained.

"Was what a lie?"

"What you said about me not being your enemy."

She hesitated for a moment and tried to collect her turbulent emotions before she answered the question. "At first, I did think of you as the enemy. I thought you were taking the ranch because of what I did. But now I realize you're just a brother who loves his sister and wants to give her the home she's always dreamed of." She hesitated. "But the Holiday Ranch is my family's dream too, Corbin. It's been in our family for over a century. It's our heritage."

"A heritage your family carelessly lost. If I hadn't taken it from them, someone else would have. Someone who would have probably kicked them out without a backward glance and bulldozed the house and barn to put up wind turbines."

It was true, but that didn't make it any better.

"But at least it wouldn't have been you." She didn't know where the words came from. They surprised her as much as they seemed to surprise him. He went perfectly still. She waited for him to say something—to question her words like she was questioning them. But he didn't. He just stood there looming over her, holding her hand and radiating heat that warmed her like a cozy fire on a dreary rainy day.

She was reminded of another night. A night when she'd stood on her front porch and stared at the same face. An intense face that gave nothing away . . . except the vulnerability in his eyes. Like that night, she made a choice. A choice she had no business making.

She leaned in and kissed him.

His lips were as soft as she remembered. They hesitated for only a startled breath before they opened and he took over the kiss.

She had thought her schoolgirl memory had made Corbin's kisses more than they were. She was wrong. She hadn't kissed a lot of guys in her life, but she'd kissed enough to know that kissing was an art very few men took the time to study.

But Corbin had studied it. He seemed to know exactly how to angle his head to make their lips fit perfectly and how much pressure to apply and how much tongue to introduce.

He didn't tug her into his arms or push her up against the door. He didn't grab her butt or slide a hand over her breast. He just stood there holding her hand and tipping her world on its axis with the skilled slide of his lips and heated strokes of his tongue. When he finally drew away, it was a struggle to keep standing. There was no way she could deal with all the conflicting emotions that swirled around inside her. So she tugged her hand free and fled into the trailer.

Once the door was closed, she rested against it and listened to the wild thumping of her heart and the sound of his truck driving away.

Chapter Eleven

"If I'd known how grumpy you were going to be, I'd have given another man the pleasure of escorting me."

Corbin pulled out of his thoughts and glanced over at Mrs. Stokes, who was sitting in the folding camp chair she had him put in the back of his truck when he and Sunny had picked her up for the Memorial Day picnic.

She wore a dress that hit her mid-calf, hose, and low-heeled dress shoes. In honor of Memorial Day, or possibly due to the heat, she had forgone her mink stole and instead had a red, white, and blue scarf tied around her shoulders. Her dyed red hair was styled in a huge bubble around her wrinkled face.

A scowling face.

He couldn't blame her for being mad. He hadn't been the best of escorts. His mind kept wandering back to Belle's kiss. What really pissed him off was that he'd been in this exact position before. After Belle had kissed him the first time, it had taken him months to stop thinking about it. Yes, he'd been hurt and angry over the twin switch, but his hurt and anger had been mixed with something else.

A heavy dose of lust.

He had thought it had to do with him being a randy teenager.

He realized now that wasn't the case.

It was Belle.

Belle bewitched him with her kisses.

"So you want to tell me why the glum face?" Mrs. Stokes asked. "As far as I can tell, you have everything a Texas man could want. Loads of money. A ranch. And two stunning women on a date."

Sunny leaned over from where she sat on the quilt and socked him hard in the leg. "Yeah, Cory, what more could you want?"

Damned if an image of Belle didn't pop into his head, which made him scowl even more.

Mrs. Stokes snorted and set down her paper plate that had once been piled high with fried chicken, potato salad, deviled eggs, and homemade sweet pickles, but now just held bones. "Come on, Sunny, let's go find ourselves some pleasant men who will let a woman take a smoke if she damn well wants to."

"Don't you dare." Corbin pointed a finger at her. "You gave me your word."

"That was when I thought I was going to be with a man who knew how to entertain me with his business knowledge and dry wit. But you've been as boring as that clown over there trying to juggle three Hula-Hoops."

Sunny set down her own plate and got to her

feet. "You're right, Fiona. Let's go find ourselves some entertaining cowboys who know how to have a little fun." She sent him a sassy smirk as she pulled Mrs. Stokes away.

"No smoking!" he yelled after them. "You either, Sunny." He spotted Tay diving at Mrs. Stokes' plate of leftover chicken bones. "No!" But of course, no female in his life listened to him and he had to wrestle the chicken wing away from the kitten.

"Good you got that away from her. Cooked bones aren't good for animals."

He glanced up to see Mimi standing there, her wide-brimmed hat casting a shadow over him and Tay. "Hey, Mimi. Enjoying the picnic?"

She sat down in Mrs. Stokes' chair and patted her leg. Tay forgot the chicken bone and jumped into her lap. "It's not as good as last year's. Of course, that's probably due to Sweetie and Cloe not ever hosting a big event like this before. Liberty and Belle were supposed to be in charge, but Liberty ran off to Houston and Belle is hiding out in your trailer." She glanced around. "I thought she'd come today. She never has been able to resist a celebration. It looks like she still needs some time alone."

Corbin wished he had left her alone. When he'd discovered her in his trailer, he should have turned tail and run for his life. He shouldn't have joined her in her junk-eating-movie-watching. He shouldn't have taken her for tacos. And he definitely shouldn't have kissed her.

Not that he had kissed her. She was the one

who had kissed him. But he hadn't stopped her. At least, not soon enough to keep him from having dreams about the gentle pull of her lips and wet heat of her mouth.

"You hot? You look a little flushed."

Mimi's question pulled him out of his thoughts. "I'm fine." He picked up his bottle of water and took a big slug. When he lowered the bottle, he noticed Mimi watching him with a smile on her face. "What?"

"Nothing. I was just thinking about you as a kid. You were always so focused. So intense. I thought maybe the ranch would help you relax a little." She laughed. "Of course, it didn't help my son relax either. The stress of ranching was what caused his heart attack."

Corbin was surprised. He hadn't heard that piece of gossip. "He had a heart attack? When?"

"Around five months ago."

Five months ago? Corbin knew Hank's stress hadn't been about the ranch, but about the loan he couldn't pay back. Guilt settled over him. "He's okay now, right?"

"Yeah, but he still needs to keep his stress level down. Which is why I pushed him to take a little trip. We're leaving tomorrow to go see Hallie in Austin for a few days and then up to Dallas to see Noelle."

He stared at her. "Who will take care of the ranch?"

"Well, you and Sunny, of course. I figure it will be good practice for when we leave at the end of next month."

Corbin should be happy Mimi was so ready to leave. And he was. He was also more than a little nervous about having the entire responsibility of running the ranch on his shoulders. He had learned a lot in the last week about caring for the cattle and horses, but not nearly enough. But before he could voice his concerns, Sweetie came weaving her way through the blankets of families covering the town park.

"Did Belle show up?"

"Nope," Mimi said. "And if she hasn't by now, I don't think she's going to. Why?"

"Because everything has gone to hell in a handcart. When Liberty left Cloe and me in charge of the picnic festivities, we thought it would just involve putting up a few flags and decorations and making sure there were plenty of popsicles for the kids. We didn't realize we'd have to deal with finding a replacement for a sick clown, the face painters running out of paint, the band not showing up, and the veterans—who should be getting ready to be honored at this very second—getting into an argument over what war was the toughest." She threw up her hands. "And it's just more stress than two expecting women should have to handle!"

Mimi held out Tay. "Here. Animals always take the stress away and calm people down." For once, Tay didn't nip or scratch. She just settled into Sweetie's arm as if she knew she had a job to do. "Now take a deep breath," Mimi continued. "I'm sure we can figure this out."

"I don't know how." Sweetie stroked Tay. "I

wouldn't be surprised if the veterans aren't pulling out weapons about now."

"Then they need a voice of reason." Mimi looked at Corbin. "Cory, you go help Sweetie get this figured out." He started to argue that this wasn't his problem, but she shut him down. "I mean it. Go on now."

Sweetie wasn't far off about the veterans being ready to draw weapons. By the time he and Sweetie arrived behind the gazebo where the veterans were waiting to be called on stage, there was definite hostility brewing. The Vietnam vets were ranting about Desert Storm not being a war while one really old guy was banishing his cane at another old guy and yelling about remembering the Alamo.

Corbin wasn't sure what to do, but after a few minutes of watching the chaos, he decided to treat the situation like any business meeting that had gotten completely off track.

"Silence!" he yelled. When everyone stopped arguing and turned to him, he cleared his throat. "Now I'm sure we can settle this without raising our voices."

The old guy shook his cane. "Pistols at dawn!"

Corbin blinked. "That wasn't quite what I was thinking. I was thinking we would calmly—"

"Why would we care what you're thinking?" The big-bellied guy in the biker vest cut him off. "Aren't you the asshole who stole the Holiday Ranch? If we meet anyone at dawn, it should be you, you thieving bastard!"

That seemed to consolidate the vets. They all

circled around Corbin and started yelling their agreement. Before he could calm them—or decide to get the hell out of there—Mickey Gilley showed up. The large dog came bounding out of nowhere into the group, barking and jumping on everyone with excited tail wagging.

Following the dog was Belle.

It annoyed the hell out of Corbin that his heart did a little jump in his chest at just the sight of her. The sides of her hair were pulled up in tiny clips with rhinestone butterflies and the rest of it fell around her shoulders in ebony curls. She wore a pretty blue gingham sundress that matched the flush in her cheeks.

"Gilley!" She tried to grab the dog's dangling leash, but Gilley dodged her and darted around the circle of vets . . . until he spotted Tay in Sweetie's arms. Then his eyes lit up and he raced straight for Sweetie with tongue lolling.

Corbin stepped in his path and pointed a finger. "Sit!"

Surprisingly, Gilley sat. At least long enough for Belle to grab his leash and praise the dog as if he hadn't just been racing out of control.

"What a good boy." She lavished him with ear scratches and kisses on his furry head. Corbin ignored the stab of jealousy. "What a good, good boy."

Sweetie peeked around Corbin. "Where in the world did you get that huge beast, Belly?"

"Gilley's not a beast. He's a sweetheart." Belle giggled as the dog gave her a big sloppy lick of thanks. She straightened. "He's mine. I adopted him from Melba this morning." She glanced at Corbin and smiled a bright smile that made his stomach feel like he'd swallowed a tank of helium.

What the hell?

"But I thought big dogs scared you," Sweetie said.

"Only when I was little." She gave Gilley's head a pat. "Turns out, now I love them."

"And how does Liberty feel about you getting a big dog?"

Belle's smile faded and she lifted her chin. "It doesn't matter what Liberty thinks. It's my choice. So tell me what's going on. Mama called me and said you needed help in a bad way."

"That's an understatement," Sweetie said as Corbin took Tay from her. "When I told Liberty I'd help her out, I didn't realize how stressful event planning is. The band didn't show up, the clown got sick and we had to find a fast replacement, and now the veterans are about to do battle. And I just can't deal with it."

Belle placed a hand on her sister's shoulder. "You go sit down and have yourself a nice glass of sweet tea. I've got this." As soon as Sweetie left, Belle moved right into the middle of the veterans and pinned on a bright smile. "Hey, y'all! For those of you who don't know me, I'm Belle Holiday. I spoke to each and every one of you on the phone a few weeks back. I'm so pleased you agreed to be here today. Wilder is one lucky town to be blessed with so many honorable and courageous men and women who had served our country so proudly. And speaking of proud,

I know everyone here is as proud of y'all as I am and can't wait to honor you on this beautiful Memorial Day. Thank you for your patience and kindness to your fellow veterans and for reminding us of what true heroism is."

The vets all exchanged guilty looks.

"Now let's get this show on the road, shall we?" Belle handed Corbin the leash before she took the man with the cane's arm. "As our oldest and most celebrated hero, you'll go first, Mr. Wazowski."

Corbin didn't know how she did it, but she got all the veterans up on the stage and through the ceremony without one thrown punch. As soon as she stepped off the stage, Cloe was there with another Memorial Day disaster and Belle was off again to deal with it . . . leaving Corbin to handle her overgrown, misbehaving mutt.

If Gilley wasn't trying to jump up and eat Tay—or more like lick her to death—he was tangling the leash around Corbin's legs, or grabbing chicken off people's plates, or stealing the pacifier right out of Tammy Sue's toddler's mouth, or lifting his leg on Mrs. Stokes' camping chair.

Of course, Mrs. Stokes didn't seem to care. Nor did any of the other folks. It was hard to get mad at a dog that looked like a huge fuzzy Muppet. Even Tay didn't seem to mind Gilley. When the dog finally ran out of energy and flopped down on the quilt, placing his big head on Corbin's leg right next to where Tay was sleeping, the kitten merely opened one eye for a second before she went back to sleep.

"I never took you for an animal person," Mrs. Stokes said as she licked her red, white, and blue Popsicle.

"I'm not."

She looked at Tay and Gilley. "You could've fooled me."

He scowled. "Where's Sunny?"

"She's enjoying her day with Casey Remington."

Corbin stiffened, causing Gilley to lift his head and look around for danger. "She'll get involved with that country Casanova over my dead body."

"Casey's not that bad. And I don't think you'll have a choice if that's what Sunny wants. She doesn't strike me as the type of woman who lets other people tell her what to do. And speaking of women with minds of their own, Belle certainly has found her gumption."

He followed Mrs. Stokes' gaze to the woman he'd been trying to avoid looking at for the last hour—unsuccessfully. Belle was talking to the clown and no doubt giving him a pep talk like she had the veterans or a scolding like she had the band that had arrived late. He had never realized how good she was at managing people. Probably because Liberty had always monopolized people's attention. Liberty got her way by being dynamic and strong willed. Belle got her way too. Just in a quieter, more subtle way.

Which explained a lot.

After watching her today, he was no longer confused about why she didn't see him as the enemy. Once again, she had tricked him. Using her bright smiles, sweet words, and hot kisses, she had snuck under his defenses and bent him to her will. And her will was to get her family's ranch back. She had made it perfectly clear only minutes before she had kissed him.

The kiss had only been part of her plan.

Well, it wasn't going to work. He wasn't going to be played by the Holiday sisters again. He intended to make that perfectly clear.

He got up and handed Tay to Mrs. Stokes. "Could you keep an eye on Tay. I'm going to take Belle her dog."

Gilley was thrilled to get back to his master. He tugged on the leash and tried to move Corbin along faster to get to Belle who was still talking with the clown.

"I'm just amazed you've never clowned before, Josiah. And it was just so sweet of you to offer to help out when Twinkles caught a cold and couldn't do it. But maybe instead of juggling Hula-Hoops, you could have a Hula-Hoop contest with the kids and give the winner a Hula-Hoop as a prize. That way the kids can all get involved, instead of just watching."

The clown hesitated for a second before he nodded. "I guess I could do that."

"Great!" She hurried back on stage and made the announcement that a Hula-Hoop contest was starting before she rejoined Corbin and took Gilley's leash. "Sorry I left you with Gilley." She leaned down and took the dog's huge head in her hands. "Were you a good boy, Mickey Gilley?" She looked up at Corbin. "Was he?"

"He was fine."

She straightened and smiled brightly. "See. Adopting him wasn't a bad decision."

Since he wasn't there to talk about Gilley, he didn't reply. "We need to talk."

A blush stained her cheeks. "I guess this is about the kiss."

Since she hadn't spoken softly, he glanced around before he took her arm and led her behind the gazebo. Once there, he released her and crossed his arms over his chest.

"I know what you're doing. You're doing to me exactly what you've done to the veterans and that clown. You're trying to manipulate me with your sweet talk and your bright smiles. But I'm not a clown, Bella. I was played by you and your sister once, but I won't be played again."

Her eyes widened. "Me kissing you had nothing to do with me trying to manipulate you."

He snorted. "Oh, come on. Tell that bullshit to someone else because I'm not falling for it. You played me in high school and you're playing me now. But I'm not a horny teenage kid anymore who will let you confuse him with hot kisses."

She blinked and he realized what he'd said.

"Not that our kiss was hot. I've had much hotter." *I've had much hotter?* He mentally rolled his eyes. *What the hell?* She had him reverting to teenage lingo.

She studied him for a long moment before she spoke. "Well, I haven't."

It was his turn to blink. "What?"

"I've never had a kiss as hot as yours. And maybe

that's why I couldn't help kissing you again. You might think it had to do with manipulation, but that's just not true. I would never think that giving you a kiss would change your mind about the ranch. I know you can't be swayed that easily. I also know you're not interested in me and never have been. You said yourself that you never settle for second best. And I've always been second best to Liberty. And even if you were actually interested in me, nothing good would come of us starting something. You're taking my family's ranch and I'm the girl who tricked you in high school."

Her eyes softened. "But you need to know that kissing you wasn't a trick, Corbin. Not on the porch of my family's farmhouse and not at the trailer. Both times, I kissed you because I wanted to." She tugged the leash. "Come on, Gilley."

She walked away, leaving Corbin feeling like a clown juggling a bunch of Hula-Hoops.

Chapter Twelve

I MIGHT HAVE MADE another bad choice.

This thought popped into Belle's mind as soon as she sat up in bed and saw the disaster Gilley had made of the room. The floor was littered with an empty Flamin' Hot Cheetos bag, a water bottle that had been completely flattened, one of her high heels covered in teeth marks, a long trail of toilet paper that led all the way down the hall from the bathroom, a tube of Crest Ultra White that was leaking toothpaste from puncture holes, and a pair of her panties ripped to shreds.

Amid the mess sat Gilley with his tail thumping against the floor and Cheetos dust clinging to the fur around his mouth and a look that said, "Hey, Mom, did you see what I did?"

Belle sighed. "I guess that's what I get for not putting you in the crate at night like Melba told me."

As if she'd just praised him, Gilley took a flying leap onto the bed and knocked her back to the pillows, covering her face with sloppy kisses that had her giggling.

Okay, so maybe she hadn't made such a bad choice.

Her cellphone rang and she held Gilley back so she could grab it from the nightstand. It was Mimi. Her grandmother had been checking on her at least twice a day since she'd moved into Corbin's trailer.

"Good mornin', Mimi." She giggled again when Gilley licked her ear.

"You sound like you're in a fine mood this morning. I gather you're enjoying living at Corbin's trailer." Mimi paused. "I saw you two talking yesterday at the picnic."

Belle's face filled with heat. Why had she told Corbin she'd wanted to kiss him? She could have just let him continue to think she was manipulating him to get the ranch. But, no, she had to be honest. Of course, the upside was that he hadn't believed her.

And why did that hurt so much?

"I guess you two are getting along better," Mimi said.

Belle adjusted the pillows and leaned back on the headboard. "Not at all."

"Hmm? He did look a little upset when you two were talking." Mimi paused. "You do seem to be upsetting a lot of people lately. Have you talked with your sister?"

"Which one?"

"Don't play dumb with me, Belle Justine. You know which one. Whatever argument you and Liberty had you need to get over it and call her."

"Why me? Why not Libby? I'm always the one who gives in first. This time, she needs to."

"Because Liberty has always been the stubborn one while you've always been more levelheaded. And you can't hide in that trailer forever."

"I'm not hiding. I showed up to help with the Memorial Day picnic."

"And that was real nice of you. Cloe and Sweetie don't know a hill of beans about event planning. I hope you're going to help them with the rest of the events while Liberty is gone."

Belle had already decided she would. She couldn't let her two expecting sisters be stressed out. That, and she missed the chaos of her job. She'd thoroughly enjoyed the Memorial Day picnic . . . even after Corbin had accused her of trying to trick him with hot kisses.

Hot kisses.

Her stomach tingled at just the thought of him thinking her kisses were hot.

"And I have another job for you." Mimi cut into her thoughts. "You need to make sure everything is okay at the ranch while your daddy, mama, and I are visiting Hallie and Noelle."

"What? You're going to visit my sisters now? Why wouldn't you wait until July after . . ." She let the sentence drift off, but Mimi finished it for her.

"We're kicked off the ranch."

"I don't think Corbin will kick you off the ranch, Mimi. But you did tell him you're going to leave at the end of the month. And I know you'd never go back on your word."

"You're darn right I wouldn't." Mimi hesitated. "But Corbin could still have a change of heart."

Belle knew her grandmother was hoping for a miracle and she hated to burst her bubble, but she couldn't allow her to keep hoping for something that wasn't going to happen.

"Corbin isn't going to change his mind, Mimi. If you could see the pictures Sunny drew of the ranch, you'd understand why. Sunny has dreamed about living on the Holiday Ranch for a long time. Corbin is only giving his sister her dream." She thought the information would help her grandmother to see the truth. She should have known better.

"The ranch is big enough to fulfill a lot of families' dreams, Belle. Including ours. We just need to keep the faith. Now are you going to come check on the ranch while we're gone or not?"

"I don't think Corbin would appreciate my help." That was putting it mildly. "He doesn't trust me."

"He doesn't trust a lot of people. After his childhood, you can't very well blame him. But that doesn't mean you give up on him. That's exactly what his parents did. Corbin needs to know there are people in this world that will be there for him no matter what."

"Fine. I'll check on the ranch while you're gone. But are you sure Daddy shouldn't stay and just you and Mama go see Hallie and Noelle? Sunny and Corbin aren't ready to start taking care of a ranch."

"I guess we'll see, won't we? Now I need to go

finish packing. I'm planning on taking both of your sisters some potted flowers. They might live in big city apartments, but that doesn't mean they can't enjoy the glory the good Lord made. When I get home, I'll bring you some to plant in front of the trailer."

"No, thank you, Mimi. I'm planning on moving out of the trailer today." She had no intentions of staying there when Corbin thought she was manipulative and untrustworthy. Nor did she plan on going out to the ranch and checking on things. She would call Sunny and make sure everything was okay. Corbin she planned to steer clear of.

It was late afternoon by the time she had packed all her things, fed Gilley and taken him for a long walk, and changed the sheets and cleaned the trailer. She was headed to Tito's Tacos to get some fish tacos before she decided what hotel to check into when her cellphone rang. She didn't recognize the number, but since it had a Texas area code, she answered it. Corbin's deep, panicked voice took her by surprise.

"I need your help."

"What happened?"

"It's Sunny. She fell getting off her horse and I'm here at the county hospital."

"Oh my God. Is she okay?"

"Do you think I'd be at the hospital if she were okay?"

Sunny's voice came through the speaker. "Yes, because you're a controlling, overreacting fool! I'm fine. It's just a little sprain."

"I'm not overreacting. We won't know it's only a sprain until the x-rays come back," Corbin said. "Either way, we won't be back to the ranch in time to take care of Tay and the horses."

As much as she didn't want to help Corbin after what he'd accused her of, she couldn't leave horses and a kitten to go hungry.

"I'll take care of them," she said. "You just worry about Sunny."

There was a long pause before he spoke. "Thank you, Bella. Tay's in the laundry room and her food is in the pantry."

It was weird to arrive at the ranch and not have someone coming out of the house to greet her. But Gilley didn't seem to mind. As soon as she let him out of the car, he raced in circles like he'd just found doggy heaven. Worried he was going to get into something, like Mimi's garden, Belle put a leash on him and walked him around so he could get used to all the different smells.

The horses were in the back pasture. When Gilley saw them, he immediately started barking and carrying on. They completely ignored him, but Belle figured it would be best to tie the dog up in the barn while she got them into their stalls and fed and watered them.

Once that was finished, she untied Gilley and headed for the house. Not trusting him with Tay, she got him a bowl of water and left him in the kitchen while she checked on the cat. Unfortunately, as soon as she opened the laundry room door, Tay streaked between her legs.

"Tay!" Belle raced after her, but Gilley got to

her before Belle could. He excitedly jumped around Tay like he'd been given a brand-new toy and didn't know what to do with it. He made the mistake of getting too close and received a sharp swat on the nose for his trouble.

You would have thought his nose had been sliced completely off by the way he squealed and skittered back against the stove, staring at Tay like she was the worst kind of assailant. Tay, on the other hand, showed no fear. She merely stood in the middle of the floor with her back arched, daring the dog to come closer.

Gilley didn't. After only a few seconds, he placed his head on his paws and fearfully watched Tay drink water from his bowl as Belle prepared the kitten some dinner.

Once she'd fed Tay, she put her back in the laundry room before going out to the car and getting Gilley's food. But the dog refused to take a single bite. He just stood at the laundry room door and whined until Belle let Tay back out. Then, once again, he kept his distance and watched the kitten play with a little crochet mouse.

Belle laughed. "So all you needed was a cute feline to make you behave."

Gilley looked at her as if to say "cute"?

Belle could have put Tay back in the laundry room, collected Gilley, and left. She'd done what she needed to do. But the country values her mama had instilled in her since birth kicked in. When someone was hurting, physically or emotionally, you always made them food.

So she pulled a frozen casserole from the freezer

and popped it into the oven before starting some drop biscuits. In Houston, she and Liberty never had time to cook. They usually grabbed takeout on the way home from the office. But that didn't mean they didn't know how. While they were growing up, Mama had made sure all her daughters helped out in the kitchen.

Belle had forgotten how much she enjoyed it. After putting the biscuits in the oven with the casserole, she chopped up some vegetables for a salad. She was making a lemon Dijon mustard vinaigrette when a car pulled up in front. Only moments later, Corbin and Sunny came in. Besides crutches and a wrapped ankle, Sunny looked fine.

If not a little ticked off.

"I swear I'm going to smother you in your sleep, Cory, if you don't stop mother-henning me."

"I'll stop mother-henning you when you stop being so careless." He pulled two chairs out from the table. "Now sit down and put up your foot."

Sunny flopped down in the chair and put her wrapped foot on the other. "I wasn't being careless. I was dismounting when that flock of pheasants spooked Sadie Mae. My foot twisted in the stirrup before I could get it out."

Corbin ran his hand through his hair. He looked like he'd been through hell. "You're lucky that horse didn't drag you all over the countryside. You could have been . . ." He let the sentence drift off and looked like he was about to pass out.

Wanting to lighten the mood, Belle spoke up.

"Is anyone hungry? There's sausage and rice casserole and biscuits in the oven." Corbin finally turned his attention to her.

"You cooked dinner? I didn't ask you to do that?"

Sunny groaned. "What my socially inept brother means, Belle, is thank you. We appreciate it."

Corbin cleared his throat. "Thank you." He glanced around. "Where is Tay?"

Belle looked down where Tay had been playing with the toy, but the kitten was gone . . . and so was Gilley. "She was just here a second ago with Gilley."

Corbin's eyes widened. "Gilley? You brought that wild dog with you?" He hurried out of the room and she followed after him.

"I'm sure they're fine. Tay put him in his place right away."

He searched the living room. "So you decided it was okay to leave her alone with him? Have you lost your mind?"

Her temper flared. "Hey, I was doing you a favor."

"My cat ending up in your dog's stomach is not a favor." He headed up the stairs.

Worried that might be the case, she hurried after him. They found both Tay and Gilley in Belle's old bedroom, now Corbin's room. The kitten was lying in the top compartment of her cat condo with half her body dangling out the little window as she batted at Gilley's wagging tail. The dog had somehow squeezed into the lower compartment. All you could see was his tail, a pile of fur, and two soulful eyes.

"What the hell?" Corbin said.

Sunny crutched into the room and laughed. "It looks like you overreacted again, big brother."

He turned to her with a concerned look. "You shouldn't have walked up those stairs without my help."

Sunny looked at Belle and shook her head. "He's hopeless. Now let's eat! I'm starving." Belle started to make her excuses, but Sunny stopped her. "Oh, no, you're not leaving me to eat alone with my overprotective brother. He'll want to serve me in bed. You were nice enough to make dinner. It's only right you should stay and help us eat it."

Since Belle hadn't eaten anything since breakfast and was starving, she gave in. That and Gilley flat refused to come out of the cat condo. When Corbin tried to pick up Tay, he got a scratch.

"Stubborn females," he grumbled before leaving the room.

Belle thought dinner would be awkward. And it would have been if not for Sunny. She was the complete opposite of her somber brother. She was talkative and funny and sweet . . . and loved embarrassing her brother.

". . . I kid you not. He wanted to be a magician when he was eight and he was horrible at it. He did this card trick where you picked a card and he tried to guess what it was. He guessed wrong every single time, but he kept guessing until he finally pulled the right one out—even if it took going through the entire deck." She winked at him. "But you did look cute in that cape you made out of Mom's black satin negligee."

Corbin's cheeks turned bright red. "I'm sure Belle doesn't want to hear about the stupid things I did as a kid."

Belle smiled. "Actually, I do." She had always thought his life had been so dismal. She was glad to know he'd had happy moments.

"He even asked for a white rabbit for Christmas that year," Sunny continued. "But Daddy was allergic to animal dander so Cory got a stuffed one instead. Which was a good thing because when he swept off his top hat to show it was empty that stuffed rabbit went sailing."

Corbin got up. "Enough magician stories. You need to lie down and rest." Amid her protests, he lifted Sunny and carried her out of the room.

While he was gone, Belle cleared the table and started washing the dishes. She was drying the salad bowl when Gilley came racing into the room and jumped up to greet her with kisses. She set the bowl down and hugged him close, pressing her face into his soft fur that smelled a little like Flamin' Cheetos.

"I can do the dishes."

She looked up to see Corbin standing in the doorway holding Tay. His scowl was back and she figured she'd overstayed her welcome.

"I didn't mind helping. You just need to wash the casserole dish." She walked over and picked up her purse. She dug around in the side pocket until she found the key to the trailer and set it on the kitchen table. "Thank you for letting me stay at your trailer. I really appreciate it."

He looked at the key and then at her. He started to say something, but then merely nodded.

When she and Gilley got outside, she led him to some bushes so he could do his business. But he didn't seem to like their scent because he only gave them a couple sniffs before he started to whine.

"Fine. I'll let you off the leash, but don't dawdle. Or get anywhere near Mimi's garden. You think Tay is tough, she's nothing compared to my grandmother."

"You can say that again. You don't mess with Mimi."

She looked up to find Corbin standing on the porch steps, cradling a sleeping Tay in his arm. Why did the sight always make her heart feel tight?

"You don't want to stay at the trailer because of its bad condition or what I said at the picnic?" he asked.

She kept her gaze on Gilley who was taking his good sweet time finding a spot to pee. "I like the trailer. It's cozy."

"So it's about what I said."

"I'm not going to stay in your trailer when you think I'm trying to manipulate you to get this ranch. Like I said, I don't want my family to have to leave a home they love, but unlike some people, I won't do underhanded things to accomplish my goals."

He came down the steps of the porch. "I didn't

do anything underhanded. Your daddy knew the conditions of the loan."

"Well, I didn't do anything underhanded either. I just kissed you because—"

"You wanted to. So you say. But why? Why did you want to?"

She didn't have an answer for that so she took the offensive. "Why did you kiss me back? Because you did kiss me back, Corbin Whitlock. Both times."

He was close now. So close she could see the five-o'clock shadow covering his jaw and the frown that tipped down his lips. And his eyes. His intense eyes that always made her feel breathless . . . and want to kiss him.

"You'll stay here tonight," he said.

She stared at him. "What?"

"You'll stay here. You're right. The trailer isn't big enough for you and a huge dog."

"I didn't say that."

He turned and whistled. Gilley lifted his leg before he came running. He jumped up on Corbin and gave him a sloppy kiss that made him laugh. "Okay, okay. You can sleep in Tay's condo."

"Now wait just one second," Belle said. "I'm not staying here."

Corbin looked at her, his gaze intense. "Why not? Are you afraid if you stay you'll want more than kisses from me, Bella?"

She willed the tingle in her tummy away. "Absolutely not."

"Then what's the problem? It's not like we'll be sleeping in the same room."

Just the thought of sleeping in the same room with Corbin had the tingle returning tenfold. She had two choices. Confess, not only to Corbin but also to herself, that she had somehow become infatuated with him. Or act like staying the night was no big deal.

"Fine. But only because it's late and the hotels are probably full. So staying would be a smart choice."

Corbin turned and muttered something under his breath that sounded an awful lot like . . .

"Sorta like licorice ice cream."

Chapter Thirteen

CORBIN WOKE FEELING groggy and annoyed.

He hadn't slept well, and it was his own damn fault. What was he thinking inviting Belle to spend the night? Had he lost his mind?

No, just his guts.

The thought of her staying in a disreputable hotel wasn't the only reason he'd insisted she stay at the ranch. He was terrified of staying at the ranch without someone who knew what they were doing. Not for himself, but for Sunny.

He was the one who had caused his sister's injury. The one who insisted on stopping to rest in a nest of pheasants. If Hank or Jesse, or any of the Holidays, had been there, they would have known better and Sunny wouldn't have gotten hurt. Corbin couldn't chance her getting hurt again . . . even if he had to put up with Belle until Darla, Hank, and Mimi got back.

Or until he could find himself a foreman.

He didn't know why he hadn't thought of it before. Probably because he'd been so tied up in proving he could become the next Clint Eastwood. Sunny getting hurt had been a reality check. He needed help if he wanted to own a ranch. Experienced help. He would start looking for a foreman today.

A whine had him rolling to his other side. A big furry head rested on the mattress only inches away. Soulful hazel eyes, that looked more human than dog, stared back at him. Corbin hadn't really wanted the dog sleeping in his room. He'd only offered to get Belle to stay. But as soon as they entered the house last night, the dog had streaked up the stairs and stuffed himself into Tay's condo. The kitten usually slept on a pillow right next to Corbin. But as soon as he'd placed her on the pillow, she'd jumped off the bed and scaled to the top of the condo where she'd spent the entire night.

The cat/dog relationship was weird to say the least. Especially when Gilley seemed to be terrified of the kitten. And yet, he couldn't seem to stay away. Maybe he just thought it was safer to keep his enemies close.

Corbin reached out and scratched the dog's head. "Smart dog."

Gilley whined again. Realizing he wasn't going to get any more sleep, Corbin got up and pulled on a pair of jeans. Tay was still sleeping peacefully so he left her and headed down the stairs with Gilley.

The sun was just peeking its head over the horizon when he stepped out on the porch. Corbin had to admit it was a pretty sight to see the pink-tinted land—his land—stretched out for as far as the eye could see. After Sunny had gotten hurt, he'd started to worry that he'd made a big mistake. He still worried. But the sight of the sun rising over the ranch caused those worries to fade away.

As Gilley raced down the steps to take care of his morning needs, Corbin raised his arms over his head and stretched, enjoying the feel of the morning breeze on his bare chest.

A soft exhalation had him freezing mid-yawn and turning.

Belle sat on the porch swing in a short white nightie that showed off her long legs. Her hair was mussed and her eyes sleepy like she'd just rolled out of bed. As his gaze wandered over her, he realized that's exactly what she'd done. She'd just rolled out of bed. A bed that had been only a short walk down the hall from where he'd slept.

"Good mornin'." Even her voice soundly sleepy and sexy.

Sexy?

Where had that word come from? And once there, it didn't want to leave. Probably because it was the exact word to describe the woman sitting in the swing cradling a mug in her hands.

Sexy.

Sexy as hell.

His morning erection grew. He lowered his arms and quickly turned his attention to the dog taking a poop in Mimi's flower garden. Belle must have followed his gaze because she jumped up from the swing and got after him.

"No, Gilley!"

The dog finished doing his business and trampled a row of flowers as he headed up the steps to exuberantly greet Belle, spilling whatever was in her mug in the process.

Concern took over sexual desire and Corbin quickly pulled the dog down by his collar. "Did you get burned?" His gaze swept over the coffee-splashed nightie. Except his attention wasn't held by the brown stains as much as the shady outline of two nipples. Two very pert nipples.

"I'm fine," Belle said. "My coffee wasn't hot."

Hot?

Yes, he felt hot. It was a struggle to talk, let alone pull his gaze away from those two sweet buds veiled beneath soft white cotton. All he wanted to do was lower his head and take one into his mouth—to wet that thin material until it turned to tissue paper beneath his tongue and he could feel the pout of soft flesh and sweet hardened nip—

Gilley's cold nose rammed into his stomach, snapping him out of the fantasy, and he quickly lifted his gaze, hoping Belle hadn't caught him staring at her breasts.

She hadn't.

Mainly, because she'd been busy staring at him.

Her gaze was burning a hole into his pectoral muscles. Her empty cup dangled from her fingers. Her lips were slightly parted. And her chest, with those tempting sweet nipples, rose and fell with each rapid breath she took.

Talk about being hot.

Corbin felt like he'd just been dropped into

a vat of hot coffee and was drowning. The only way to save himself was to reach out and grab on to the woman in front of him.

He started to do just that when the screen door squeaked open and Sunny's voice rang out.

"Good mornin'!"

Corbin swung around so fast he tripped over Gilley and ended up stumbling back into Belle. She lost her balance and sat down hard in the swing. He followed, sprawling onto her lap and setting the swing into motion. He sat there for a few stunned seconds, enjoying the feel of soft sweet breasts against his back, before he sprang to his feet and turned to her.

"Are you okay?"

Her cheeks were a flaming pink that rivaled the vine flowers that grew on the porch railing.

She cleared her throat. "I'm fine."

Well, he wasn't. He wasn't fine at all. Before either woman noticed the hard-on bulging the fly of his jeans, he turned and headed down the porch steps.

"I'm going to check on the horses."

"Remember Hank's rule?" Sunny said. "No goin' in the barn without boots."

"That's true," Belle said. "Going barefoot to the barn isn't a good idea."

Annoyed that not only his sister was telling him what to do, but also Belle, his reply was snappish. "Well, Hank doesn't make the rules anymore. I do. If I want to go out to the barn without boots, I'll damn well go out to the barn without boots."

But he soon realized the reason behind Hank's

rule. While feeding the horses, he ended up stepping in horseshit. As he was trying to wipe his foot off on some straw, he stepped on a rusty horseshoe nail. It was lying on its side and didn't break the skin, but it still hurt like hell. It was a struggle not to limp back to the house.

Thankfully, Belle had gone inside and Sunny was the only one sitting on the porch. Although he soon realized he shouldn't be thankful for that.

"So do you want to explain what's stuck in your craw this morning?"

"There's nothing stuck in my craw." He grabbed the garden hose and sat down on the porch steps to wash his feet.

Sunny got up and crutched over to the top of the steps. "Okay, let me rephrase that. What's going on between you and Belle? And don't you dare say nothing. Because it wasn't nothing that was going on when I stepped out on the porch this morning. You two were staring at each other like frostbite victims looking at tubs of warm bathwater."

Sunny had always been good at analogies. That's exactly how he'd felt. Like Belle was a bathtub filled to the brim with perfectly warmed water and all he'd wanted to do was sink deep inside her. Of course, he wasn't about to admit that to anyone.

"You must not have been fully awake if that's what you saw."

"Oh, I was fully awake. And what I saw on your face was exactly what I saw a hundred times before. You were looking at Belle just like you used to look at Liberty."

That got his attention . . . and scared the hell out of him. He might be able to deny what had been happening on the porch to his sister, but he couldn't deny it to himself. He had felt something this morning. Something similar to what he'd felt the other night when Belle had kissed him. But it wasn't like the infatuation he felt with Liberty. It was just lust because he'd gone so long without sex. That was it. Nothing else.

"I don't know what you saw, Sunny, but I'm not interested in the Holiday twins—either one." He finished rinsing off his feet and got up to shut off the hose. When he turned back to the porch, Sunny was looking at him with concern.

"Are you sure you haven't taken your infatuation with Liberty and turned it on Belle? Because Belle isn't Liberty, Cory."

"I figured that out a long time ago, Sunny."

"Then why did you insist she stay here?"

He knew in order to get the concerned look off her face he'd have to be truthful. "Because ranching isn't as easy as I thought it would be and Belle knows her way around the ranch."

She stared at him for a long moment before a grin spread over her face. "So you talked her into staying because you're scared?"

"Not scared. I just need her help until Hank gets back."

The grin got bigger. "Are you admitting you're not a rancher, Cory?"

He climbed the steps until they were eye level.

"I'm not a rancher . . . yet. But I will be with a little more practice."

"Well, you won't be getting any help from Belle. She told me she's planning on leaving this morning." She hesitated. "Probably because my brother was looking at her like she was a deep-basted turkey and he was a stray, starving dog."

"Very funny. You have to talk her out of leaving."

"Me? I'm not the one who's scared of running the ranch alone." She sent him a smug smile before she crutched her way into the house, leaving Corbin to follow behind and try to figure out what to do. He would walk across a bed of rusty horseshoe nails barefooted before he told Belle he was scared.

Luckily, while he was getting dressed, Rome called to ask if he wanted to help with the branding and it gave Corbin the excuse he needed to keep Belle from leaving. As soon as he ended the call and finished getting dressed, he walked down the hall to her room. She answered the door dressed in a T-shirt, jeans, and boots. Why had he been hoping for the thin white nightie? He mentally shook the image from his mind and pinned on a smile.

"Great. You're ready."

"Ready? For what?"

"Rome just called and says he needs help with the branding. Since he's family, I figured you'd want to help too."

"I can't. I need to find a place to stay."

There was something about the stubborn set of

her jaw that said she was determined to stand her ground. Which meant he needed to try another tactic.

"Okay, well, I guess I can figure out how to get to the Remington Ranch by myself."

"Wait, Sunny's not go—oh, of course she's not. Her ankle." Her face scrunched up with concern and he knew he had her.

"It's fine. I can figure it out. You do what you need to do." He turned to leave, but only got two steps before she stopped him.

"I'll go with you."

Chapter Fourteen

CORBIN'S RIDING HAD greatly improved since the last time Belle had seen him ride. He no longer looked tense and awkward. In fact, all the way to the Remington Ranch, he sat in the saddle as if he'd been riding for years instead of just a few weeks. One hand lightly held the reins while the other rested on his thigh and occasionally reached up to pat Homer's neck.

Belle struggled to keep her eyes off him and he seemed to be having the same problem. Every time she glanced over, he was watching her . . . and no doubt thinking the same thing she was: what the heck had happened on the porch that morning?

She'd thought it was his kisses that left her all shaky and flustered. But as soon as he stepped out on the porch without a shirt on, she'd felt like leaves trembling in a strong wind.

Corbin had a phenomenal body. The type of body without an ounce of fat. Just stacked muscles one upon the other. When he lived in Houston, he must have worked out at a gym. A lot. He had a toasty tan as if he'd been working the ranch shirtless. When he'd raised his arms over his head to stretch, her tummy had taken a dip at the sight of the pale skin of his armpits covered in dark hair. He had looked so virile standing there stretching with his hair all bed messed that it had taken her breath away.

She was still having a hard time breathing.

Which was why she shouldn't have agreed to come with him. But she couldn't in good conscience let him ride to the Remington Ranch alone. Not only could he get lost, but also hurt. He might have gotten better at riding, but he still wasn't an expert. This was proven a few minutes later when a rabbit raced out of its hole and spooked Homer. The horse jumped sideways, almost tossing Corbin off.

"You might want to keep a hand on the saddle horn," she said. "Horses are unpredictable."

He tightened his hold on the reins and placed his other hand on the saddle horn. "How long have you been riding?"

"Since I was four."

He flashed a glance over at her. "Your daddy put you on a horse when you were only four years old?"

"No. Mama didn't want us riding until we were six. It was Liberty who thought we should learn to ride at four. I helped her get up on our old plow horse first and then she pulled me up. Thankfully, Betsy didn't move very fast. She plodded along at a snail's pace no matter how hard we kicked our bare feet and wanted her to go faster."

"You didn't have on boots?"

"Nope. And that's another thing we got a stern lecture for . . . along with not putting a saddle on Betsy."

"Hank didn't spank you?"

"Never." She glanced at him. "Did your daddy spank you?"

He was silent for so long that she thought he wasn't going to answer. "My daddy didn't care enough to discipline us. We were nonentities to him."

Belle knew he and Sunny had been passed around to different relatives, but she didn't know all the details. She couldn't help being curious. "And your mama?"

Again, there was only the sound of creaking saddle leather and horse's hoofs hitting the hard earth before he spoke.

"Mama had a big dream of what a family should be. But since she only ever loved one man—and that man was a two-timing loser—that dream was hard to obtain. Which didn't work out so good for me and Sunny. When she found out about Daddy fooling around with another woman, she'd kick us all out. Then when he came back, she'd want the dream again and she'd come and get us at whatever relative she'd pawned us off on."

The story was so tragic Belle didn't know what to say. No wonder he wanted to give Sunny a stable home. She had never had one . . . and neither had Corbin.

"I'm sorry," she said.

"It wasn't that bad. It certainly wasn't as bad as

Jesse's childhood. Sunny and I weren't physically abused."

Just mentally.

And Jesse was physically abused? Liberty had told her that he was adopted, but not about the abuse. No wonder Liberty was so protective of him. She had always championed the underdog. Not that Jesse was an underdog. It looked like he had overcome his abusive childhood and become a successful man who had found happiness.

An image of Jesse's big smile as he showed her the loft he'd renovated for her and Liberty flashed into her head and she felt like the worst person in the world. He'd only been trying to do something kind for her and the woman he loved and Belle had been rude and childish.

Was still being rude and childish.

She might not think he was the best man for Liberty, but that wasn't her choice. And it certainly didn't give her the right to be mean to him. She had always prided herself on being kind to others, but she hadn't been kind to Jesse. And if anyone needed extra kindness, it was someone who had lived through abuse.

Whether physical like Jesse or mental like Corbin.

Which might explain why, when they reached the branding corral, Belle suddenly found herself taking on the role of guardian angel. Corbin couldn't move without her issuing a warning.

"Corbin! Watch out for that closing gate."

"Corbin! Don't get too near that steer's horns!"

"Corbin! Back up when they release that calf from the chute!"

Thankfully, he listened. But so did every other cowboy in the corral. Later in the afternoon, Casey Remington came over to tease her. Casey had always been a big tease.

"Looks like Belly has a bo-o-oyfriend. And here I was hopin' I could be your boyfriend now that you're back in town."

"Sure you were." She rolled her eyes before she went back to watching Corbin help herd the cows into the pen. She felt a little more relaxed now that he was on horseback.

"Are you questioning my sincerity, Belle Holiday?"

"Yes, I am, Casey Remington."

"I'm wounded."

"I'm sure you're just devastated."

Casey rested his arms on the rail she stood at and leaned over, blocking her view of Corbin. "If you'd take your eyes off your boyfriend long enough to look at me, you'd see the hurt in my eyes." His eyes held nothing but a teasing twinkle. She couldn't help but laugh and tease back.

"You're right. You do look devastated. And we can't have that, now can we? No woman in Wilder would ever want Casey Remington's heart to be broken. So of course, I'll be your girlfriend. In fact, why don't we just cut through all the dating nonsense and get to the good stuff."

His eyes lit up. "Sex?"

"Marriage."

The disappointment in his eyes had her laughing again. "Are you sure you just don't want to stick to the sex?" he said. "Sex with me is the good stuff."

She swatted the brim of his hat. "Noelle might be right. You are arrogant, Casey Remington."

He winked. "It's not arrogance when it's the truth."

"Well, that's something that's never gonna be proven, Lover Boy. At least not with me." She tugged his hat over his face before shoving him out of her way. When her gaze found Corbin again, she discovered he had stopped herding cows and was looking in her direction.

"Everything okay?" she yelled.

He nodded before he wheeled Homer around and headed out of the corral with the other two cowboys. Belle had to hand it to him. He might not be as experienced as the rest of the branding crew, but he was a fast learner. And a dedicated one. No matter what job Rome gave him, he did it.

And Rome gave him some pretty difficult jobs. Especially since he was a greenhorn.

"Are you trying to kill him, Rome?" she couldn't help asking when her brother-in-law walked past her.

Rome shrugged. "He wanted to be a rancher. I'm just showing him what he's in for."

Since ranching was hard, she couldn't argue the point. Nor could she help feeling sorry for Corbin as they rode back to the Holiday Ranch. He looked like he'd been rode hard and put away wet. She understood. She hadn't worked half as hard as he had and she was about ready to drop out of her saddle. The hot afternoon sun beating down on them didn't help.

When she spotted the cluster of trees up ahead, she couldn't help veering toward them. For a man who got lost easily, he seemed to have figured out the way home.

"Where are you going? The ranch is the other way."

"I want to show you something." She took the lead. When they got to the trees, she issued another warning. "Watch out for low-hanging branches."

"I've listened to you telling me what to do all day. I'm kinda over it."

"Fine. Don't be careful, but don't blame me if you get knocked off your horse."

"And I thought Liberty was the bossy twin," he grumbled.

She laughed. "That doesn't mean I can't be bossy too."

"So . . . what was Casey Remington talking to you about?"

"He was just being Casey. He's a world class flirt."

He snorted. "You didn't look like you objected."

She glanced back at him in surprise . . . and ran into a low-hanging branch.

"Be careful of low-hanging branches," he said with a definite smirk in his voice.

When they broke through the trees, Corbin released his breath in a startled gasp. She understood. Cooper Springs was gasp worthy. The water was clear as glass and the cypress trees surrounding the springs were huge, green, and majestic. It was like stepping into a magical world.

"Damn," Corbin said. "I heard you and Liberty talk about swimming at Cooper Springs, but I pictured it more of a watering hole for cattle."

"During droughts, cattle did come here to drink. The rest of the time, Daddy kept the herd away so us girls could have our own private swimming hole." She dismounted and tied the reins to some mesquite scrub before she toed off her boots.

"What are you doing?" Corbin asked.

"What does it look like I'm doing? I'm going swimming."

"Oh, no, I'm not skinny-dipping with you, Bella."

"I'm not skinny-dipping with you either." She stopped pulling off her socks and glanced up at him. "Unless you aren't wearing underwear."

"I'm wearing underwear."

"Then what's the problem?" She peeled off her shirt. She had on a sports bra that covered her as well as, if not better than, a bikini top. Although the material of her panties was a little thinner than bathing suit bottoms. So after pulling off her jeans, she wasted no time diving in. The cold water was a little startling, but also refreshing. She resurfaced with a gasp of pleasure.

Corbin was still sitting on Homer.

"You should get in," she called. "It feels heavenly."

"No, thanks. I'll just head back to the ranch."

"Suit yourself."

He went to turn the horse, but then stopped. "You swim well, right?"

She knew how protective he was of Sunny, but having that protectiveness focused on her made her smile. "Not as good as Liberty, but okay."

"What's okay?"

"Are you worried I'm going to drown, Cory?" It was the first time she'd used his nickname. She liked the way it sounded. Corbin was rigid and uncaring . . . but Cory was the man sitting on the horse looking concerned. The man who heaved a heavy sigh and dismounted before he started removing his clothes.

Belle should have looked away.

She didn't.

Just like she had done earlier that morning, her eyes ate up the naked flesh Corbin revealed as he turned away from her and drew his T-shirt over his head. His back was just as tanned and muscled as his chest. Those muscles stretched and flexed as he finished taking off the shirt and neatly laid it on the nearby rock. After he removed his boots and socks, he lowered his jeans to reveal black boxer briefs that covered hard butt cheeks she could have bounced a quarter off of. His legs were as muscled as his back, chest, and arms, but not as tanned. They were paler and covered with a light dusting of dark hair.

He turned and Belle's mouth went dry.

He was either extremely well endowed . . . or extremely excited. Before she could figure out which, he dove into the springs. He came up a few feet away from her and slicked back his hair with one hand. Water droplets clung to his dark lashes and slid down his nose and high cheekbones. One drop quivered on his bottom lip. An overwhelming desire to tread closer and lick that drop off settled in her stomach. Before she could do something stupid, he spoke.

"Are you satisfied?"

She knew he was talking about her getting him into the springs, but the question held more meaning to her. Was she satisfied? The answer came quickly.

No, she wasn't satisfied.

Yet.

Chapter Fifteen

THIS HAD TO be the worst idea ever.

As soon as Belle started taking off her clothes, Corbin should have gotten the hell out of there. Instead, he had watched as she'd peeled off her shirt to reveal the sexy-as-hell lavender sports bra that crisscrossed the pale skin of her back and was so thin he could see the points of her nipples.

But the worse agony had been watching her jeans slide down those mile-long legs and seeing the way her panties rode high on those two perfectly curved butt cheeks. He almost swallowed his tongue when she moved toward the springs and the satiny material rode even higher. Desire had punched him hard in the stomach and not even diving into cold water had softened the throbbing hardness between his legs.

He wanted Belle. He couldn't argue the point anymore. He wanted her like he had never wanted another woman before in his life.

Not even her sister.

Liberty had been a teenage crush. The stunningly beautiful homecoming queen he, and every other hormonal boy at Wilder High, had fantasized about. But he realized now that he'd never known Liberty.

He didn't know what kind of snacks she liked. Or what kind of movies she loved to watch while eating those snacks. He didn't know what kind of ice cream she hated and what kind of tacos she preferred. He didn't know if she sat a saddle like she had been born in it and if she could get people to do what she wanted with only a smile and a few kind words. He didn't know if she was a sucker for starving dogs and a phenomenal kisser.

But he knew those things about Belle.

He had learned them over the past week.

And they only made him want her more.

But he wasn't about to give in to his desire. He wasn't about to fall under another Holiday's spell. Especially when her friendliness and kisses were all a ploy to get back her family's ranch.

And yet, there was a tiny part of him that didn't believe that. A tiny part that, when he looked into her eyes like he was looking into them now, saw something real. Something warm and honest and giving. Something that drew him like a blazing fire in the midst of a blizzard.

He just wasn't willing to trust that something.

Pulling his gaze away from her, he dipped under the water and started swimming. He didn't count how many laps he did. He just swam until his lungs hurt and his muscles ached and his cock softened. And the belief that Belle felt something real for him disappeared.

When he finally grew too exhausted to continue and came up for air, he discovered Belle had gotten out . . . she just hadn't gotten dressed. She was stretched out on a large flat rock at the edge of the springs drying in the sun like a breathtaking sun goddess. Her arms were stretched above her head and one knee was bent and her ebony hair spread out on the rock like spilled ink.

He got hard all over again.

Which pissed him off.

Uncaring that he had a boner he could hollow out and use as a canoe, he waded to the shore. "What the hell are you doing?"

Belle lifted up to her elbows and looked at him. "Drying off before I put my clothes back on. You should probably dry—" Her eyes lowered and she cut off mid-sentence. Her lips opened on a puff of surprise.

"Yes," he said. "I have one hell of a hard-on and isn't that what you were shooting for? Take Corbin Whitlock to Cooper Springs and see just how worked up I can get him."

She sat up and stared at him as if he'd just sprouted horns. "That's not why I brought you here at all. I brought you here because I thought you'd enjoy a swim after you worked so hard. I did not bring you here to be insulted." She started to get off the rock, but he grabbed her arm and stopped her.

"Then explain the show you put on of stripping off your clothes, making sure to tease me just enough with your tempting hard nipples and sweet curvy ass. And then when that didn't get my attention, you stretched out on this rock like some kind of seductive sun goddess."

She stared at him. "Seductive sun goddess?"

He snorted. "As if you don't know how seductive you are. You've been trying to seduce me since you got here—trying to use your flirty smiles and sultry looks to drive me crazy." He pointed a finger at her. "But I'm telling you right now, Bella. You aren't going to succeed." As if of their own accord, his eyes lowered to her mouth. "I'm not going to give in and taste those sweet lips." His gaze lowered even more. "I'm not going to touch those tempting breasts. Or cup your sweet ass. I'm stronger than that. Much stronger."

But if that was so, why couldn't he turn and walk away? Why was he just standing there with desire and need pulsing through his body and his heart thumping like a trapped rabbit's?

"Well, I guess I'm not that strong," she said in a soft whisper. When he lifted his gaze, her mismatched green eyes were dark and needy. He only had a chance to draw in a startled breath before she kissed him.

She kissed him like a woman who knew exactly what she wanted and wasn't afraid to go after it. Sliding both hands in his hair, she fisted her fingers and held him tight as she greedily stroked his mouth with her tongue.

Like a lit fuse that finally reached its detonation point, all the want he'd been holding back exploded and he realized he wasn't strong enough either. He no longer cared that this was just part of her plan to get her family's ranch back. All he cared about was keeping her sweet lips on his.

When her legs opened and encircled his hips, he groaned and slid his hands to her butt, caressing the full sweet flesh before he lifted her off the rock and pulled her flush against his needy body. He loved the way her bare skin felt on his, the brush of her long legs and the press of her hot center. He loved the melting of her breasts on his chest and the curve of her ass cheeks in his hands.

But he needed to feel more.

He wanted to cradle the soft fullness of her breasts in his palm and feel her pouty nipples against his tongue. He wanted to strip her completely naked and stretch her out on the rock and worship her like the goddess she was.

Unfortunately, sports bras weren't easy to get off.

Especially wet ones.

The stretchy material seemed to be superglued to her body. He struggled to even get his hand under it, let alone get it off. As he tried his best to figure it out, he felt her smile against his mouth and drew back to find her eyes twinkling and her lips quivering with suppressed laughter.

"It's not funny." But he couldn't help smiling when she lowered her legs and leaned against his chest in a fit of giggles. He tugged at the thick elastic band of the bra. "Come on. Help me out here. How do you get this thing off?"

She drew back and blinked at him innocently. "Are you saying you need help undressing a woman, Corbin? I thought you did everything well."

"I do." When she lifted her eyebrows, he conceded. "I need help. Please."

Her smile was almost blinding as she reached down and grabbed the edge of the sports bra. In his defense, it was even difficult for her to get off. With her arms bent and crossed in front of her, she had to wiggle and squirm her way out.

"Speaking of help," she said.

"Absolutely not. I'm having too much fun watching."

Fun was the wrong word. He groaned when her breasts popped out of the lavender material. They were small and perfect with the plumpest-looking nipples he'd ever seen in his life. Before she had even gotten the bra over her head, he had them in his hands and his head lowered. She sucked in a startled breath when his lips first touched her and then released it in a soft sigh when he pulled the sweet bud into his mouth.

As he suckled, she flung off her bra before she drove her fingers through his hair, pressing him closer. She didn't need to hold him. He had no intentions of going anywhere anytime soon. He sipped and tongue-stroked until her nipple was tight and hard before he turned his attention to the other breast. When he finally lifted his head, it was to find Belle's eyes glazed over and her breathing heavy and erratic.

He felt damn happy that he was responsible.

But he wasn't finished.

Not by a long shot.

He slipped a finger into the elastic of her panties, but then stopped. "You okay with this, Bella?"

"Please," she said in a breathy puff of air.

He closed his eyes in thanks for a second before he lowered her panties. After she stepped out of them, he lifted her back to the rock. "Is it too hard? Because we can move to the grass."

She shook her head and drew him in for another kiss.

"Good," he whispered against her lips. "Because I want to see you stretched out naked in the sun like the goddess you are."

She made a sexy mewling sound deep in her throat that had him growing even harder. But it was nothing compared to how hard he got when she stretched out on the rock like a fuckin' sun goddess. She was so damn beautiful it took his breath away. All he could do was stand there and allow his gaze to greedily run over her from the tips of her perfectly lined-up toes to the top of that wealth of ebony hair.

Hair the same color peeked out from the juncture of her mile-long legs. A thin line that held his gaze and drew him closer. But he wasn't ready to touch her there yet. There was so much more he wanted to explore first. Every inch of her sun-warmed skin intrigued him.

He took his time, allowing his hands to go where they would. They wanted to touch her everywhere. The smooth slopes of her shoulders and the full hills of her breasts. The soft skin over her rib cage and the cute dip of her belly button. The sexy curves of her hips and the toned muscles of her thighs.

He had told Sunny only hours earlier that he

wasn't infatuated with either twin, and he hadn't lied. He wasn't infatuated. He was obsessed.

But only with one twin.

This twin.

He had once thought Belle was the insecure, unassuming follower who did whatever her sister commanded. But the woman stretched out before him wasn't insecure and unassuming. She was confident and brazen and sexy as hell.

And his . . . at least for the moment.

A moment he didn't intend to waste with too much thinking.

He slid his hands down her thighs until he reached her knees. With just a little pressure, she spread her legs for him. The view took his breath away. He studied her moist pink center for a moment before he lifted his eyes to find her watching him. He held her gaze as he knelt and lowered his head. At his first sip, desire flooded her eyes and all he wanted to do was keep that look on her face.

Forever.

Chapter Sixteen

THIS WASN'T BELLE'S first time having sex. In college, she'd had sex with a guy she'd met in her chemistry class and dated her entire junior year. Riley had been nice and considerate. He'd asked what she liked and tried to give it to her. Unfortunately, she hadn't had a clue what she liked and Riley was too inexperienced to give her options.

That wasn't the case with Corbin.

He didn't ask her what she liked. He paid attention. His gaze never left her face as his lips, tongue, and mouth experimented. If something didn't feel right, he seemed to know immediately and he changed either his technique or rhythm. It only took a few tries before he found what she liked.

What she liked a lot.

The sweet pulls of his lips and lush strokes of his tongue made her feel like her veins had just been injected with the most mind-blowing drug. She couldn't look away from the hot cobalt blue of his eyes. Not when the tidal wave of heat had goose bumps spreading over her skin. Not when her entire body started to quiver with the intensity of her need. And not when everything inside her tightened and then released in an explosive orgasm that sent her soaring and then gently floated her back to earth.

She didn't know how long she lay there looking up at the clear blue Texas sky with a satisfied smile on her face. It took the sound of a zipper closing for her to come out of her euphoric trance. She sat up to find Corbin buttoning his jeans. Jeans that couldn't hide his impressive hard on.

"What are you doing?" she asked.

He glanced up, his hot gaze sweeping over her body before quickly looking away. "What does it look like I'm doing? Getting dressed. We should probably get back before Sunny starts to worry."

He obviously regretted what had just happened. She should too. Getting sexually involved with the man who had foreclosed on her family's ranch was just plain stupid.

And she wanted to be stupid all over again.

Not only because she'd just experienced the most amazing orgasm of her life, but also because of what he'd said before she'd kissed him. No one had ever referred to her as a seductress. A goddess. It didn't matter that he only thought she was seducing him to get back the ranch. She wanted to feel like a goddess again.

She wasn't above seducing him to get what she wanted.

Of course, he wasn't making it easy. He dressed in record time and took off before she even got her boots on. By the time she got back to the ranch, he was in the barn unsaddling Homer. He didn't even glance up when she approached the stall.

"I'll unsaddle Sadie Mae," he said. "You don't need to stay."

"My daddy taught me to always take care of my horse."

"Suit yourself." He went back to taking off the bridle.

"So that's it," she said. "You're just going to give me the best orgasm of my life and then ignore me?" His shocked eyes snapped over to her. It felt good to be the kind of woman to shock people. "And don't you dare use the excuse that I'm only using you to get the ranch back," she continued. "I know you aren't going to do that."

"Then what do you want?"

It didn't take her any time to come up with an answer. "More of what you gave me today."

He blinked before he looked away and ran a hand through his hair. "That's not a good idea, Bella."

"Why not? I'm not asking you to marry me, Corbin."

He looked back at her, his eyes confused. "What is with you Holidays? Don't you know I'm the enemy?"

"You didn't feel like much of an enemy today." She sent him a sassy smile before she led Sadie Mae into a stall.

She wasn't surprised to find him gone once

she'd finished taking care of Sadie. Nor was she surprised to find him waiting on the front porch with her suitcases.

"I guess I've overstayed my welcome," she said as soon as she reached the porch.

He held out the key to the trailer. "Like I said before, you can stay at the trailer for as long as you'd like." She knew he wanted to add, just as long as you aren't near me. He was obviously running scared and she couldn't help but feel happy. She was making Corbin Whitlock, a savvy tough businessman, nervous. Talk about feeling empowered.

She tried to hide her smirk as she accepted the key. "Feel free to stop by anytime."

His brow knotted. "I won't."

For some reason, she didn't believe him.

Gilley was quite happy to be back at the trailer. While Belle took a shower, he had a party—getting into the leftover tacos she'd gotten for dinner, chewing up a pair of panties, and shredding an entire roll of toilet paper. After she cleaned up the mess, she put him in his crate.

"Obviously, I need to get you a cat to keep you in line."

Once Gilley was settled, she headed for bed. As soon as she slipped beneath the covers, her mind filled with thoughts of Corbin and Cooper Springs. He wanted her. It was obvious he wanted her. It was also obvious that he still thought she was trying to play him. He had said as much before he had called her a seductive goddess and completely wiped out any logical thoughts in her head—like that having sex with a man who didn't trust her was an extremely stupid idea.

And yet, if she had thought logically she wouldn't have had the best orgasm of her life. She wouldn't know what it felt like to be worshipped with soft kisses and hot sweeps of a skilled tongue.

Corbin had worshipped her. Damned if she didn't want to be worshipped by him again.

A pounding on the door had her sitting straight up in bed and Gilley barking like crazy from his crate. She jumped up and headed to the living room where she peeked out the front window. It was dark, but not so dark she couldn't see Corbin's big white truck. A giddy feeling settled in her stomach as she soothingly talked to Gilley to quiet him before she answered the door.

Corbin stood on the other side looking like he'd just rolled out of bed. His hair was mussed like he'd been running his fingers through it, his western shirt wasn't snapped correctly, and he was barefoot. He looked totally confused. Like he didn't know how he'd gotten there.

"What game are you playing, Belle? Tell me. What game are you playing?"

She used the same soothing voice she'd used with Gilley. "I'm not playing a game, Corbin. I swear—"

He didn't let her finish before he stepped in and kissed her. His kiss was as desperate as his voice had been. His lips were hot and greedy as he shoved the door closed and pushed her against it. His hands seemed to be everywhere at once— sliding under her pajama top and cradling her breasts. Slipping into her pajama bottoms and cupping her bottom. Skimming her back and caressing her stomach. Strumming her nipples and brushing heated strokes between her legs.

"I tried," he whispered against her lips. "But I can't fuckin' resist you anymore. Let me stay, Bella. Please let me stay."

She shouldn't. He still didn't trust her. Any good relationship needed trust. Relationship? Is that what she thought this was going to turn into? If that was so, she needed a reality check. She and Corbin could never have a relationship. He had made it clear he had no intentions of giving back her family's ranch. Once he kicked her parents and grandmother out, her entire family would hate him.

But was it wrong of her to want just one night?

She drew back from the kiss and looked into his eyes. "Stay."

He closed his eyes for a second as if offering up a prayer of thanks before he lifted her into his arms and carried her to his bedroom. On the way past Gilley's crate, he spoke.

"It's okay, boy. I'm not gonna hurt her."

Belle wished she could believe that.

But whether he hurt her or not, she hadn't lied. She wanted him to stay. She wanted it more than Flamin' Hot Cheetos or Pea-Nutty Buddy muffins or fish tacos. He was an addiction she couldn't resist.

When they got to his bedroom, he became less desperate. His kisses were slower and deeper. His touches gentler and more thorough. He had her naked before she knew what was happening. Then he lowered her to the mattress on the floor and started taking off his clothes. It was too dark to see anything. And she very much wanted to see everything. So she reached over and turned on the lamp sitting on the floor next to the mattress.

He froze in the middle of pushing down his jeans.

"You got to see me," she explained. "I want to see you."

A spark of amusement flickered in his eyes before he finished taking off his jeans and kicking them away. He had already removed his shirt so all he had on were his boxer briefs. Briefs that barely concealed the hard length beneath. That length sprung out when he pushed down the elastic waistband. Belle couldn't help but stare.

It was impressive.

Or maybe what was impressive was how well it fit with the rest of Corbin's hard, muscled body. He reminded her of the sleek stud horse her father had paid a pretty penny for.

Corbin was a stud.

And he was hers to ride... at least for one night. She wasn't about to waste a second being inhibited. As soon as he stepped closer, she reached out and wrapped her hand around his hard length. His eyes registered surprise, then steamy heat. As she learned the feel of him, his breathing escalated and he made satisfied, sexy noises in the back of his throat. Wanting to satisfy him even more, she knelt on the mattress and kissed the very tip.

His eyes opened and he looked down at her with a look so hot it took her breath. "You don't have to, Bella."

"I know. I want to. You told me yourself that I needed to try things."

He blinked before a smile tipped the corners of his mouth. She didn't think there was anything more beautiful than Corbin's smile. "Then by all means. Try me."

As soon as she took him into her mouth, his breath left his lungs in a rush and his entire body trembled. His reaction made her feel empowered, but also protective. He had been through so much pain in his life, all she wanted to do was give him pleasure—to erase all the bad memories and replace them with good ones.

So, with deep pulls of her lips and long strokes of her hand, she went about giving him the same amazing orgasm he had given her. By his groans and trembles, she seemed to be doing a good job. But before he could climax, he pulled away. She started to argue and then only gasped when he dropped to his knees, pushed her back to the mattress, and spread her legs.

Using his scorching mouth and tongue, he had her reaching orgasm so fast she didn't know what happened. Her insides were still quivering by the time he put on a condom and entered her. The deep stretch had her body filling with need once again as if it hadn't just found release.

"You okay?" His passion-thick voice brushed her ear.

Too overwhelmed for words, she nodded.

He slowly pulled out, angled his hips, and then thrust in much deeper. He continued to take his time with slow, deep thrusts that touched an erogenous spot she'd just discovered. When she couldn't take it anymore, she slipped her hands over his muscled butt cheeks and urged him to go faster.

He got the message and rode her hard and fast.

"Bella." He whispered her name like a song. An anthem. A prayer. A word that didn't need anything else with it. It was complete just by the way he said it.

She met every thrust, the friction fanning the fire he'd built inside her. She was almost there when he groaned and tensed.

"I'm sorry, Bella baby. I can't hold back." With a sexy growl, he came. She tumbled right after him, never looking away from the gorgeous sight of him finding his release.

At that moment she knew. She knew she would never ever experience what she had just experienced with anyone else. And that wasn't good. Especially when he didn't seem to feel the same way. He didn't look into her eyes and share in the feeling. He didn't brush a kiss over her forehead. He didn't pull her into his arms and hold her close. He just got up and walked out of the room. A second later, she heard the toilet flush and water running.

She didn't know why she was upset. His reaction after giving her an orgasm at Cooper Springs had proven Corbin was a flight risk. But he could have at least given her a kiss or a thank you. Or anything. Knowing him, he would just walk out the door without a word.

She wasn't about to let that happen.

She got up and grabbed the first article of clothing she found on the floor. It happened to be his western shirt. She was snapping it haphazardly when he walked back into the room.

"What are you doing?"

She blinded at his naked body. God, he was a phenomenal male specimen. "What are you doing?"

"I was throwing away the condom."

"Oh. I thought . . ."

"I was leaving?"

"Well, it was what you did earlier today."

He pulled her into his arms and nibbled his way along her neck. "I'm sorry. I was just . . ."

"Scared?"

He drew back, his eyes serious. "I still am."

She knew how hard that was for him to admit. She cradled his face in her hands. "Well, you don't need to be. I promise to go easy on you."

A smile spread over his face. "You will, huh? What if I don't want it easy?"

"Then I guess I'll have to give it to you rough."

He laughed. "I don't think there's anything rough about you, Belle Holiday."

"Is that so?" Using a technique Hallie had taught her, she hooked her foot behind his ankle and shoved hard. He stumbled back and she took advantage of his instability to dive on him and knock him back to the mattress. Once they had stopped bouncing, she straddled him with a triumphant smile.

"Then I guess you don't know me as well as you think, Corbin Whitlock."

Chapter Seventeen

"You're making me extremely nervous," Corbin said as he watched Belle lean out the open hatch of the hayloft.

She glanced back over her shoulder and sent him a sassy smile. To say she looked stunning with her ebony hair flowing around her shoulders and her naked body highlighted by the blue sky and the afternoon sun would be an understatement. She looked like a fantasy come to life.

His fantasy.

How many times in high school had he thought about this exact scenario? Being naked in the Holiday Ranch hayloft with a dark-haired beauty. Back then, he had wanted that beauty to be Liberty. But now, he only wanted Belle.

"I'm just trying to see where Gilley is." She leaned a little farther out and his heart dropped.

"Dammit, Bella!" He got up from the blanket they'd spread on the hay and pulled her away from the opening and into his arms. It never failed to amaze him how well she fit.

"You are such a worrywart." She looped her arms around his shoulders. "Do you know that?"

"I do." He kissed her. She melted into the kiss just like she had melted into his arms. He started to lower her back down to the blanket, but she stopped him.

"We don't have time. I have to go into town and meet with Tammy Sue about her daughter's birthday party."

"I thought you were taking time off." He kissed his way down her neck. As always, she smelled like sunshine and lemons.

"I was, but I can't let my pregnant sisters take on all the town's events. The Memorial Day picnic proved event planning is too much for them and Liberty won't be back until Monday."

"Actually, she and Jesse are coming back today." He filled his hand with a soft naked breast and groaned with pleasure. But that pleasure was short lived when she pushed out of his arms.

"Today? They're coming back today? But what about the Grossmans' wedding in Houston?"

"Jesse said the bride cancelled it last minute."

Belle looked horrified. "And Liberty didn't try to talk her out of it? Danielle really loves Joshua. She just got cold feet and needed to be talked down from her panic."

Corbin sighed because it looked like he wasn't going to get another roll in the hay. Which was probably for the best since he had a pile of work he needed to get done—not to mention horse stalls to clean out and foreman resumes to look over.

He grabbed his boxers and pulled them on. "I don't think talking people down from their panic is Liberty's forte. That's yours, Bella. Which is why you two make such a good team. Liberty is the assertive businesswoman who won't take crap from anyone and you're the—"

"Weak doormat."

He glanced at her. "I was going to say the sweet negotiator. The one who makes everything come together and run smoothly without a hitch. Liberty might be a vocal leader, but leaders can't lead without a strong wingman. Or woman in this case."

"You think I'm strong?"

"One of the strongest women I've ever met."

A bright smile spread over her face. "I am pretty strong."

"Hell yeah, you are. You certainly brought me to my knees last night." Her entire body flamed a pretty pink and he couldn't resist dropping the jeans he'd just picked up and pulling her back into his arms. "Don't tell me you're embarrassed about what you did, Bella. Because you certainly didn't act embarrassed last night, my brazen lioness."

She beamed. In the last few days, he'd come to realize how much she loved being called empowering names. And he loved how she took on the roles.

"Brazen lioness?" She scraped her nails over his back, sending heat straight to his groin. "Maybe you would like to feel my claws."

"I'd love to feel your claws."

She showed him more than just her claws. She used her teeth and her tongue to drive him absolutely wild. When he was on the edge of oblivion, she straddled him and rode him hard and fast. She seemed to love being on top and he certainly didn't have a problem with it.

"I think I like the lioness as much as the goddess and the siren," he breathed when they had both found release and were cuddled together. A sniff had him tensing. When hot tears hit his chest, he completely panicked. "Bella." He lifted her chin to find her green eyes watery and her cheeks wet. "What's wrong, baby? What happened?"

She swallowed hard. "She didn't even call to tell me she was coming home."

"Oh, Bella." He pulled her back in his arms. "Don't cry. I'm sure Liberty feels just as hurt about your fight as you do."

"She has a funny way of showing it."

He sighed. "I hate to admit it, but Liberty is a lot like me. We keep our emotions close to our vest. When someone hurts us, we completely shut down. That's what I did when my mama kept dropping me off with relatives. I just shut down and acted like I didn't care." He hesitated. "But I did care. Liberty cares too. We're just not like you and Sunny. Y'all wear your emotions on your sleeves and that's not a weakness. It's a strength. So why don't you just do what you really want to do and go see her? I know she'll be happy you did."

She lifted her head. "You think so?"

He smoothed back her hair. "I know so. When Sunny and I fight, I'm secretly happy when she shows up and refuses to let me sulk."

A smile tickled the corners of her mouth. "You are a sulker."

"Just one of my many flaws."

The smile faded and she reached up and cradled his jaw in her soft hand. Something entered her eyes that made his heart tighten and his breath get locked in his chest. "You don't have that many flaws, Corbin Whitlock. You like to make people think you do, but I know better. I know underneath that tough exterior is a soft heart that when it loves, it loves completely. If your mama couldn't see that, then that's her problem not yours."

That soft heart felt like it was swelling right out of his chest.

Which scared the hell out of him.

He forced a laugh. "Boy, do I have you fooled. Now come on, let's get dressed. You have a sister to go see."

He volunteered to keep Gilley, but the dog whined so much when Belle went to get in the car that she ended up taking him with her. Corbin knew how the dog felt. As he watched her car drive away, he wanted to whine and chase after it.

What had she done to him?

The last few days, he had thought of every excuse he could think of to get her out to the ranch—something was wrong with Homer, Mimi's tomato plants looked like they might be dying, he bought some new flowers to replace the ones Gilley had trampled but didn't know how to plant them. At night, he thought of more excuses to show up at the trailer—he'd left something he needed for work, he wanted to make sure the air conditioner was working, he accidentally bought dog treats for Tay and thought Gilley would like them.

He knew Belle saw right through his excuses, but she never said a word. She just showed up at the ranch or welcomed him into the trailer. That was just who she was. She was a giver.

He, on the other hand, was a taker.

He was taking from her. He knew he was taking. But he couldn't seem to stop. She filled the hollow emptiness inside him. An emptiness he had ignored all his life. Now that he knew how it felt to feel full, he wasn't sure if he could ever live with the emptiness again.

And what if he didn't have to?

The question dropped into his head out of nowhere like a thousand-pound barbell. It jarred him, causing him to tense and wake up Tay who was sleeping in his arm.

"I've lost my mind, Tay," he said as he stroked the kitten's head. "If I'm actually considering making things serious between me and Belle."

The kitten blinked her blue eyes at him as if to say, "And you aren't already serious?"

He sighed and ran a hand through his hair. "Damn. How do I think this is going to work? Do I think she's just going to smile and bear it when I kick her family off their ranch?"

Again Tay stared at him and he what she was thinking.

"Oh, no, I'm not taking on all the Holidays."

Except as soon as he spoke the words, he realized he'd already taken on all the Holidays. Hank, Darla, and Mimi were living under his roof. And Belle was living in his—

"No!" He shook his head adamantly. "Absolutely not. Belle has not taken over my heart. I'm letting good sex make me think things I have no business thinking. I'm not in love with Belle. I like her—I like her a lot. But I don't love her." He pointed a finger at Tay. "Got it?"

Tay only stared back.

Frustrated with his thoughts, he headed inside and spent the rest of the day working on anything and everything to keep his mind off Belle. It didn't work. No matter how busy he was, thoughts of her drifted in.

It was a relief when Sunny, who had gone into town for groceries, came home in the late afternoon and walked into the office. Her sprain had healed and she was back to being as feisty as ever.

"Whatcha doin', big brother? Besides making loads of money for me to spend."

"I'm looking through foreman resumes."

Her eyes registered surprise as she flopped down in a chair across from his desk. "You're hiring a foreman? What happened to my brother who thought he could handle a ranch by himself?"

"He figured out that it's harder than he thought. And since the end of the month is fast approaching and Hank, Darla, and Mimi will be leaving soon, I figured it would be a good idea if we had an expert taking over."

She stared at him. "So you're still going to kick them out?"

"I'm not kicking them out, Sunny. They knew the terms of the loan."

She hesitated. "And what about Belle?"

He gave an innocent shrug. "What about her?"

She rolled her eyes. "Did you really think I wouldn't figure out what you two have been up to?"

"We haven't been up to anything. Belle has just been helping out while her parents and grandma are away."

"And where have you been going for the last couple nights?"

"I told you. To have a drink at the Hellhole."

Sunny threw up her hands and huffed. "Good Lord, Cory. You must think I was born yesterday. I know you've been going to the trailer to see Belle because I followed you last night." He went to interrupt, but she stopped him. "Before you go all postal on me, you aren't the only one who worries about your sibling. I worry about you too. I warned you about getting involved with Belle, but it looks like you didn't pay me a speck of attention. You never pay me a speck of attention. Which is why I'm thankful to have Jesse as a brother now. At least he listens to me."

That hurt. "I listen to you. But I'm a grown man and you have no business following me around."

"Really? Just like I'm a grown woman and you had no business hiring that security team in Paris to keep tabs on me?"

She wasn't supposed to know about that. He

cleared his throat. "That's different. You were a young woman in a foreign country. All kinds of things could have happened to you."

"That's bullshit, Cory, and you know it. I get that you love me. I get that you worry about me. I appreciate you taking care of me when we were kids. I didn't have a mama and daddy to love me, but I had you. And I'm grateful for all you went without so I could have everything. But I'm a grown woman now. I don't need someone watching my every move and making all my choices. I need a brother who trusts me to make my own choices."

"Fine. Make your own choices." He turned the laptop to her. "You want to choose the foreman for your ranch, choose the foreman for your ranch."

"I don't want to choose a foreman." She hesitated. "I don't want this ranch."

He shook his head. "Don't start that again. All you talked about as a kid was the Holiday sisters and how much fun it would be to live on the Holiday Ranch. You drew picture after picture of this ranch."

"I was a kid who wanted a stable—"

"Home. Exactly. And I gave it to you."

She growled with frustration. "Dammit, Cory! Would you listen to me for just a second without cutting me off? Yes, as a kid I dreamed about having a life like the Holiday sisters. I wanted to live on a ranch surrounded by five sisters who were my closest friends and ride horses and jump from haylofts and skinny-dip at Cooper Springs."

"And you can do all those things now. Except jumping from haylofts. That's too dangerous."

She closed her eyes and took three deep breaths before she opened them. "I'm leaving, Cory."

"What? What do you mean you're leaving?"

"I mean I'm packing my bags and heading to Houston to live as a twenty-three-year-old single woman in a big city until I figure out what I want to do with my life."

"Wait a second, you can't go to Houston. I got this ranch for you."

"I thought that at first. But after seeing you here, I realize that you never got the ranch for me. You got it for you. You dreamed about this ranch, didn't you? You dreamed about living here as much, if not more, than I did."

He shook his head. "Absolutely not."

She smiled sadly. "Then you're lying to yourself. But I'm not lying to myself, Cory. I don't want someone else's dream. And that's what this ranch is. This is the Holidays' dream. Not mine. And not yours."

"Then why did you come here with me and act like this was what you wanted?"

"Because you wouldn't listen to me. So Jesse and I thought that if I went along with it and came here, you'd figure out soon enough that ranching isn't for you and head back to Houston. We didn't think you'd take to ranching like a Labrador dog to water."

Corbin stared at her. "You and Jesse? You plotted against me?"

She sighed. "Now don't get all riled up. We

thought we were doing the best thing for everyone. You'd figure out you weren't a rancher and the Holidays would get their ranch back."

"Did the Holidays know about your plot?"

She nodded. "Hank's and Rome's jobs were to show you how tough ranching is."

"And the rest of the Holidays' jobs?"

"To endear you and make it hard for you to kick them out of their home."

To endear him.

Darla's baking. Mimi's country advice and mothering . . . and Belle's seduction. It had all been to get the ranch back. He hadn't thought he would ever again feel the way he had after his mama dropped him and Sunny off with another relative. But that's exactly how he felt now.

As always, anger was the way he dealt with the pain.

Chapter Eighteen

BELLE'S STOMACH WAS a bundle of nerves as she drove down the long driveway that led to Mrs. Fields' boardinghouse. Gilley was sitting in the back seat attached to a dog car restraint Corbin had bought him because he didn't want Gilley interfering with her driving or getting hurt if she stopped suddenly.

It had been a thoughtful gift.

Corbin was a thoughtful man. She hadn't realized how thoughtful until the last few days when she'd gotten a peek at the man behind the solemn expression and vulnerable eyes. A man who was funny and clever. Hardworking and dedicated. Softhearted and caring.

She wanted to believe he cared about her. There were times, like today, when he'd looked at her a certain way, that she thought he had feelings for her. But then he'd blink and the look would be gone, leaving her wondering if it was all just her wishful thinking.

She had been doing a lot of that lately. Wishing for things that weren't very likely to happen.

And she needed to try and keep her feet firmly planted on the ground.

Or maybe what she needed to keep planted was her heart.

She kept wanting to give it away to a man who didn't really want it.

Jesse's truck and Liberty's SUV were parked in front of the carriage house when she got there. Her nerves reached an all-time high and she was debating whether or not to turn around and leave when Jesse came out the back door of the house with Buck Owens waddling behind him. Gilley spotted the pug and went crazy, whining and barking as he tried to get out.

Jesse didn't seem at all taken back by the sight of a huge dog sitting in her back seat. He grinned as she got out of the car.

"Let me guess. Melba."

"His name is Mickey Gilley."

Jesse laughed. "Of course it is." Belle was hesitant about letting Gilley out. She didn't know how he would act with other dogs and she didn't want Buck hurt. But Jesse didn't seem to have the same hesitation.

He opened the back door and received exuberant licks for his trouble. "Hey, big boy. You want to meet Buck?" He unclipped the straps and Gilley shot out of the car like a rocket and raced over to Buck. They sniffed each other for a few seconds before they started posing and playing and racing around the yard.

"That's not a dog," Jesse said. "That's a hairy pony."

Belle laughed. "A hairy pony I've grown extremely attached to."

"It's easy to do. Liberty and I don't know what we'd do without Buck."

She looked at him and he smiled that dopey smile—which didn't seem at all dopey anymore. Just sincere. With his mussed strawberry-blond hair and soulful brown eyes, he didn't look like a villain who was going to break her sister's heart. He just looked like a sincere guy who wanted Belle to like him. Which made her feel like the worst kind of villain.

"I'm so sorry, Jesse," she said.

He tipped his head. "For what?"

Obviously, he was a nice enough guy to go easy on her. But she didn't deserve the easy way out. "I'm sorry for being so rude to you and acting like a jealous brat."

"Hey, I wouldn't be so thrilled either if my sister showed up with a saddle tramp like me."

"From what Corbin tells me, you're far from a saddle tramp."

His eyes registered surprise. "What Corbin tells you? Have you and my brother become friendly?"

She felt her cheeks heat. "Umm . . . sort of. I've been helping him out at the ranch while my parents and Mimi have been visiting Hallie and Noelle."

"Well, that's real nice of you. But I hope you haven't been helping him out too much. That's not part of the plan." Before she could ask what he meant, he continued. "And speaking of helping people out." He glanced up at the second-story windows of the carriage house before looking back at her with sad eyes. "She's missed you, Belle. She's been real upset since y'all's fight."

"Upset or pissed off?"

He laughed. "Pissed off, but that's how your sister deals with her pain." He glanced at Gilley, who was exploring the yard with Buck. "Why don't you let me keep an eye on Gilley while you go up and talk to her?" He winked. "I've always been good with horses."

As she climbed the stairs to the office, Belle prepared herself for the worst. Jesse was right. Liberty usually showed her hurt through anger. It was likely she was going to explode as soon as she saw Belle. Good thing Belle had become extremely good at dealing with Liberty's anger.

When she got to the top of the stairs, she found Liberty at the coffee bar fiddling with the coffee maker. Just seeing her sister made tears spring to her eyes. Liberty must have sensed her presence because she glanced up. Belle prepared herself for yelling. Instead Liberty merely lifted a hand at the coffee maker.

"I can't get it to work."

Belle bit back a smile. Liberty had never been good with anything mechanical. "Does it have water?"

"Of course it has water. I'm not that inept, Belly."

"You aren't inept." Belle walked over and opened and closed the pod lid before pushing one of the brewing buttons. "You're just too impatient and always put the pod in before the machine says 'ready to brew.'" To prove her words, coffee poured down into the waiting cup.

Liberty sighed. "Well, damn."

All the tension evaporated and they started laughing. Deep, stomach-clutching laughter like Mimi when she'd had too much elderberry wine. When they finally sobered, they spoke at the same time.

"I'm so sorry, Libby!"

"I'm so sorry, Belly!"

They came together in a tight hug and burst into tears. Since Liberty rarely cried, seeing her sister so upset made Belle cry even harder. They stood there sobbing until Liberty finally spoke in a nasally voice.

"Unless you want snot all over your shirt, Jelly Belly, I need a Kleenex." She drew back. Her face was blotchy and her cheeks wet. Belle knew she looked just the same.

Belle grabbed one of the little napkins from the coffee bar and handed it to her before she took one for herself. They kept their arms linked as they moved over to the leather couch and sat down.

"Remember when I had a major crush on Timmy Myers," Liberty said. "I invited him out to Cooper Springs to swim and he came up out of the water with that green booger hanging out of his nose."

Belle laughed. "And that was the end of your crush."

"I just couldn't get that image out of my head."

Liberty took Belle's hand and smiled. "I missed you, Belly."

"I missed you too. I'm sorry I've been such a jealous brat. I knew one of us was bound to fall in love. I just didn't think . . ."

"It would be me."

She shrugged. "You always said you didn't need a man to make you happy."

Liberty leaned back on the couch and sighed. "I know. I thought I didn't. But then I met Jesse." She shook her head. "I didn't ever want to be some silly woman who got all sappy over a man. But dammit, I'm a silly woman all sappy over a man. I don't like it, but I can't seem to help it. I know this entire thing"—she waved a hand around—"has taken you by surprise. It's taken me by surprise too. But that doesn't mean I had the right to push you into moving here. You're right. I'm impatient, controlling, and used to getting my way."

"Because I've always wanted you to make all the decisions. You were right too. I was too afraid to make decisions for myself because I was worried they'd be wrong."

Liberty smiled. "I guess that's why we make such a good team."

"It is." She paused. "But I've come to realize we aren't always going to be a team."

Liberty sat up. "What are you talking about? Of course, we'll always be a team. We're the Liberty Belle." She held up her fist. "Together, we ring loud and clear."

Belle laughed at the motto Liberty had come

up with when they'd been eight. "That's still the worst motto ever."

"It is not. We can't ring without each other."

Belle had thought that once too. Now she knew it wasn't true. "You can ring just fine without me, Libby." She smiled with her lips . . . and with her heart. "And I can ring just fine without you."

Liberty's eyes narrowed. "What happened while I was gone?"

"Nothing happened. I just realized I can make decisions for myself."

Liberty studied her. "No, something else happened. You look different. You look all flushed and happy like . . ." Her eyes widened. "Like I looked after I fell in love with Jesse."

Damn, Belle had forgotten how perceptive her sister was. Still, she wasn't about to confirm her suspicions. Especially to herself.

"I don't love Corbin."

Liberty's eyes widened and Belle instantly realized her mistake. "Corbin? As in Jesse's half brother?"

Belle wanted to backpedal, but it was too late. Besides, she really needed to talk to her sister about everything that had happened while she'd been gone.

"Corbin and I kind of started . . ." She tried to find a word, but before she could, Liberty found it for her.

"Having sex?"

Since she couldn't deny it, she only shrugged. It was a mistake. Liberty's eyes bugged out of her head and she jumped to her feet.

"Jesse!"

Belle got up. "Please don't tell me you're going to freak out because I had sex. I've had sex before, Libby."

"Oh, it's not the sex. It's who you had it with."

Jesse appeared at the top of the stairs. "Did you need something, darlin'?"

Liberty pointed a finger at him. "You said that Corbin was a nice guy. You said all I had to do was trust you and your plan. Well, I trusted you and your plan and not only hasn't Corbin given my family's ranch back, but now he's seduced my sister. And I'm done trusting. I'm going to kill him!" She started to stride past Jesse, but he grabbed her around the waist and lifted her off her feet.

Which was the worst thing he could possibly do. Belle knew her sister, and you never used physical force with Liberty unless you wanted her to reciprocate.

"Ouch!" Jesse released Liberty and held his chest with a horrified look. "Did you just titty pinch me?"

"I sure as hell did and I'll do it again if you don't get out of my way." Liberty started for the stairs again, but this time, Gilley came charging up the stairs and stopped her. The dog jumped on her, covering her face in wet kisses. Belle didn't know if the dog thought Liberty was her or he'd just realized that there were two identical women he got to love.

"What the hell!" Liberty tried to push the dog away, but Gilley wasn't having it. He knocked her back a few steps, which had Buck—who had just made it up the stairs—growling and waddling over to protect his mama. Jesse scooped him up as Belle grabbed Gilley's collar and pulled him down.

"You need to get a grip, Libby," she said. "I'm a big girl who can handle having sex."

Liberty studied her. "I know you, Belly. You can't tell me it was only sex."

"That's all it was."

The deeply spoken words had Belle turning to find Corbin standing at the top of the stairs. His eyes were cold and hard and his jaw was clenched. For a brief second, she wondered why he was so angry, then her mind keyed in on what he'd said. Not the agreement that it was only sex, but the verb he'd used.

Was.

As in past tense.

"So you just used my sister for sex?" Liberty asked. "Is that what you're telling me? You just used her as something to keep you entertained while you waited to kick my parents and grandmother out of their home?"

He didn't blink. Nor did he look at Belle. "Pretty much."

Belle had been wondering how Corbin felt. She had her answer now. She felt like a wrecking ball had just hit her square in the chest. She had never experienced a broken heart, but that was the only way to describe the pain.

Liberty growled and started for Corbin, but

Jesse stepped between them. "What the hell, Whitty? Why would you do that? Belle's family."

Corbin laughed, but it held no humor. "Family? Yeah, sorry, but that word doesn't hold any meaning for me. Especially when it comes out of the mouth of a brother who has been stabbing me in the back."

"What are you talking about?"

Corbin's eyes glittered with anger. "I'm talking about the plan you hatched up with the Holidays to get rid of me."

Belle waited for Jesse to deny it, but he didn't. He just sighed. "It wasn't a plan to get rid of you, Whitty. We only wanted to make you realize that ranching isn't your thing."

Corbin snorted. "Please don't act like you did it for me. The only reason you did it was to get Liberty back. You don't give a shit about your own brother and sister. All you care about is getting some Holiday puss—"

"Watch it, Whitty. You're treading on thin ice."

"What? Does the truth hurt, big bro?" He laughed that humorless laugh again that made a shiver run down Belle's spine. "Well, too bad. And here's some more truth that's going to hurt. Your plan failed. I'm not giving back the ranch. I don't care if Sunny doesn't want it. Or if I'm the worst rancher this side of the Pecos. Holiday Ranch is mine. So fuck you and all the Holidays." He finally looked at Belle and smiled smugly. "Although I guess I already fucked you."

Before Belle could get over Corbin's brutal words, Jesse punched him. Corbin's head flew back, but he recovered quickly and threw a punch at Jesse. Liberty went to join the fight, but Jesse pushed her out of the way and drove into Corbin, knocking him onto the floor where they wrestled while the dogs jumped around them and barked.

Belle stood there stunned for a few seconds before she realized that if anyone was going to take control of the situation, it would have to be her. She placed her fingers in her mouth and loudly whistled. Gilley and Buck dropped to their haunches while both Jesse and Corbin stopped wrestling and looked at her.

"That's enough," she said in the voice she used when kids in a wedding party got too rowdy. She couldn't help the stab of concern she felt at seeing Corbin's swollen eye and the blood dripping from his nose. Nor could she ignore the pain that still throbbed in her chest from his hurtful words. But she pushed those feelings down and tried to keep her voice steady and emotionless. "You need to leave."

There was a flash of vulnerability in his deep blue eyes—or maybe it wasn't vulnerability at all. Maybe it was disgust. She no longer felt like she could read Corbin.

Maybe she never could.

He didn't say a word as he got up and headed for the stairs. Gilley went to follow him, but he pointed a finger and said, "Stay."

The dog stayed, but let out a pitiful whine as he watched Corbin leave.

Belle knew exactly how Gilley felt.

Chapter Nineteen

WHEN CORBIN GOT back to the ranch, he saw Hank's truck parked just outside the barn. He'd hoped he would have a little time to deal with his emotions before he had to talk to another Holiday. But that didn't look like it was going to happen.

And maybe it was for the best.

He needed his anger to get through the next few minutes.

As soon as he was out of his truck, Hank came out of the barn to greet him. He wasn't a smiling guy, but he was smiling today. "Looks like you did a damn fine job of taking care of things while we were—" He stopped in front of Corbin and his eyes narrowed. "You get in a fight, son?"

A piercing pain speared through his already bruised chest at the word son. He ignored it. "I found out about your and Jesse's plan to get me to give back the ranch."

Hank sighed and stared down at his boots. "Ahh. So I guess you aren't real happy with him or me." He lifted his gaze. "And you have every right to be mad. But just so you know, Jesse really thought you weren't cut out for ranching. I did too. In the last couple weeks, I realized our mistake. A man either has ranching in his blood, or he don't. You have it, Corbin. You might not have all the skills, but you have a love of the land. And that's the most important part of being a rancher." He hesitated. "We'll pack up tomorrow and be out of your hair by noon. I'll go tell Darla and Mama."

Corbin should be happy that Hank hadn't put up a fight. But as he watched the old cowboy walk away, he didn't feel happy. He felt sad and guilty, which made him feel even angrier. Needing an outlet for his emotions, he headed for the barn and saddled up Homer.

He didn't think about where he was going. He just gave the horse free rein to go wherever he wanted. It turned out Homer decided to take the same path he'd taken before when Corbin got lost. Corbin didn't realize it until he glanced up and saw the fuck-you tree.

It was almost like the entire ranch was flipping him off.

After only a slight hesitation, he guided Homer over to the tree.

The time capsule had been stuffed in a huge knothole in the hollowed-out trunk. Corbin had to dig through dead leaves and debris to get to the rusty old tackle box. He thought it would hold a collection of things that were popular when Belle and Liberty were kids. Instead, there were two envelopes. One with Belle's name and one with Liberty's.

He didn't care what Liberty had written. But he did care what Belle had.

Carefully, so as not to rip it, he worked open the envelope and took out the folded piece of paper. When he opened it, his heart tightened at the neat, concise handwriting.

When I'm thirty, I will be living right here on the Holiday Ranch. I will be married to Nick Jonas—sorry, Libby, I called first dibs—and Nick and me will have twin daughters who I will name after the holiday they are born closest too because that's our family tradition. (I hope it's not Halloween.) I will have a tiny little wiener dog that I will name Oscar Mayer and maybe a cat that Daddy won't make sleep out in the barn. And horses. Lots of horses. Liberty and her husband, Joe Jonas, will live here too with the rest of our family. Since that's a lot of people, Nick will build us another house close to Cooper Springs. A cozy house—cuz I love cozy—with a garden and a front porch where I can rock my daughters to sleep and listen to my husband sing the songs he wrote for me.

Moisture collected in Corbin's eyes and he took a moment to collect himself before he carefully folded the letter and placed it back in the envelope. Once the box was hidden in the tree, he remounted and headed back to the ranch. When he got there, he expected to get the cold shoulder.

He didn't.

As soon as he stepped in the door, Mimi yelled at him to wash up for supper. When she saw his swollen eye, she made him sit down and got him a bag of ice to hold on it while he ate. He wasn't very hungry, but since Darla had gone to the trouble to make him his favorite chicken and dumplings, homemade dinner rolls, and cherry pie, he forced himself to eat.

During supper, Hank talked about the ranch as if he wasn't going to lose it while Darla watched Corbin with sad eyes and Mimi cuddled Tay. When Hank ran out of conversation, Mimi finally spoke.

"I see I got some new flowers. Did something happen to the garden while I was gone?"

"Gilley."

Mimi laughed. "I figured as much." She stroked Tay's head. "I knew it wasn't my sweet girl."

That was the final straw. Corbin had about as much of their fake kindness as he could take. "It's not gonna work. I'm not going to let you stay. Especially after what y'all did."

Mimi smiled softly. "I don't blame you a bit. But I think you'll miss us. I'm sure gonna miss you."

Before he could figure out how to reply to that, the front door opened. His heart jumped and then settled in disappointment when it turned out to be Jesse. His brother looked wild eyed and distraught.

"Libby's not here?"

Darla got up, her eyes concerned. "No. Is she missing?"

Jesse flopped down in a chair and covered his face with his hands. "We got in a pretty intense argument. I was sticking up for Corbin and she was sticking up for Belle." He paused. "She broke our engagement and left me."

"So I heard," Mimi said.

Jesse lowered his hands. "Libby called you?"

"No. Cloe did."

Jesse jumped up, but Mimi stopped him from leaving. "Sit back down, Jesse. You're not going over there tonight. Liberty needs some time to cool off or you'll just make matters worse." She glanced at Hank. "Hank William, grab a couple bottles of my elderberry wine and take these boys out to the barn. I figure you've dealt with your daughters enough that you can give some good advice."

Hank looked surprised. "Me? I've never figured out how to deal with my daughters."

"Then I guess y'all will need to figure it out together."

The last thing Corbin wanted to do was go to the barn with Jesse and Hank. "I'm not—"

Mimi cut him off. "Don't sass me, Corbin Whitlock. Now git!" She glanced at Jesse. "You too."

He and Jesse got up and begrudgingly followed Hank out the door. While Hank went to the cellar to get the wine, they stood on the porch and glared at each other.

"What were you thinking seducing Belle, Whitty?" Jesse asked.

"I didn't seduce Belle." He glanced back at the house. "And keep your voice down."

"Why? If you didn't seduce her, you have nothing to be ashamed of."

"I'm not ashamed. I just don't think Belle wants her folks and grandma knowing about her sex life."

"And that was all it was? Sex?"

He looked away from Jesse's penetrating gaze. "That's what Belle said, didn't she?"

"No. That's what you said. What she said was she was an adult woman who could handle having sex. You were the one who said that sex was all it was."

"What difference does it make who said what? You and I both know it was only sex to her—all part of the plan to get me to let go of the ranch."

Jesse stared at him. "Is that what you think? You think Belle was in on—" He cut off when Hank appeared, toting three bottles of wine.

"Come on, boys. Let's go get drunk and pretend like we understand women."

Mimi's elderberry wine was as strong as Corbin remembered. After drinking half a bottle, his anger dulled . . . just not the ache in his chest. Had Jesse hit him there? It certainly felt that way. The spot beneath his rib cage hurt like hell.

He glanced over at Jesse who was sitting only feet away, leaning against another bale of hay. Corbin kicked at his brother's boot. "You sold me out, b-b-brother." The slurring of his words made him realize how drunk he was.

Jesse took a long drink from his bottle. "I did not sell you out. You couldn't even ride a horse and you w-w-wanted to be a ranch-her and neither Sunny or I could talk you out of it."

"Because I wanted to give our sister a home. Not that you give a sh-sh-shit about Sunny."

"At least I listen to her when she talks. You don't pay a speck of attention to what she wants." Jesse waved a hand at the hayloft. "This ranch is a per-f-f-fect example. She didn't want it. It was just you being a controlling, arrogant ass."

"Maybe so, but you're a lying backstabber. You acted like you cared about me. But as soon as a beautiful woman showed up, I was chopped liver."

"I love chopped liver." Hank sat on a bale of hay close to the open hatch doors, staring out at the night sky. "Darla makes this chopped liver dip that you spread on Ritz crackers. Damn, it's good." When Jesse and Corbin didn't say anything, he glanced at them and shrugged. "Just saying. Chopped liver's not a bad thing. I wish I had a brother to call me chopped liver. But I'm an only child. I never had a sibling to fight with. I get it. You both think you have just cause to be pissed at each other. And maybe you do. But you're still brothers and that means something."

Jesse lowered the bottle he'd just taken a drink from and pointed a finger at Hank. "You're right, Hank. Brothers do matter." He looked at Corbin. "I'm sorry, Whitty. I just—"

"Wanted to score points with your girlfriend and her family."

Jesse sighed. "Maybe so, but it was the right thing to do. This is their home, Whit. Not yours. Thus the name Holiday Ranch."

Before Corbin could argue the point, Hank spoke. "That's not true. Just because my name is on the ranch that doesn't mean it's not Corbin's home. Home isn't about having your name on the entrance of a ranch. Or on a title of a deed. I've learned that in the last few months. It's about finding a place you feel comfortable. A place where you want to love your woman and raise your family. A place you want to rest your head at night ... and if possible, for all eternity. Mrs. Fields' Boardinghouse will always be how the townsfolk refer to the place you bought, Jesse. But that won't make it any less your and Liberty's home. I guess it's true what people say. Home is where the heart is." He looked at Corbin. "Where's your heart, son?"

Damned if an image of Belle didn't pop into his head. He didn't want it there. But there she was ... riding through a rainstorm into the barn. Sitting on the porch swing with her hot gaze wandering over him. Standing on a corral fence yelling out warnings for him to be careful. Lying on a rock at Cooper Springs with her mismatched eyes giving him a look that took his breath away.

Hank was right.

Damned if he wasn't right.

Home wasn't about owning something. It was about a feeling. Not just of comfort, but of belonging. His parents had never given him a home, but they had given him Sunny. Sunny was his home ... and now Belle was too. She not only made him feel comfortable, she also made him feel like he belonged. She had given a home to his heart.

"Bella." Her name came out of his lips on a whisper. Just not soft enough.

Jesse looked at Corbin with sad eyes. "She wasn't in on the plan, Whitty. I swear she didn't know anything about it. After you left, she wanted all the details. When I told her, she got mad as hell."

"She got mad?"

Jesse nodded. "She said it was the worst thing Sunny and I could have done to you after what your mama did. Breaking the trust you had in us had broken your heart." He set down the bottle and moved closer until he was leaning on the same bale of hay as Corbin. "Damn, I'm sorry, Whitty. I'm so sorry." He put an arm around him and tugged him close. "I love you, bro. You're my family."

Corbin pulled him in for a tight hug. "I love you too. And I don't want the ranch. I want Belle."

Jesse nodded against his shoulder. "And I want Libby."

"Wait a second," Hank piped in. "You both want my girls?"

They drew apart and looked at Hank, speaking at the same time. "Yes, sir."

Hank sighed. "I'm sure I'll have a lot of questions for you in the morning, Cory, but right now I'm too drunk to deal with it." He got up and weaved on his feet. "So I'm going to bed."

Corbin didn't want to go to bed. He wanted to see Belle.

But getting up wasn't easy. Nor was getting

down the ladder. Although he did a better job of it than Jesse who slipped and landed on his ass at the bottom. Which caused all three men to bust out laughing. They laughed even harder when Hank fell into Mimi's garden on the way up the porch steps.

Mimi and Darla, who were sitting on the porch, didn't find it so amusing.

"Hank Holiday!" Mimi hollered as both women got to their feet. "You get out of my flower bed before I switch your bee-hind."

"I'm trying, Mama, but this soil is like quicksand."

"We got ya, Hank!" Jesse said as he grabbed Hank's hand. Corbin grabbed the other. But Hank was a big man and it took some hard tugging to get him up. Once he was standing, Darla scowled at him.

"Don't you dare think that you can come into the house covered in dirt, Hank Holiday." She hurried down the steps and started brushing him off . . . until he grabbed her around the waist and tugged her close.

"I thought you liked me being a little dirty."

Darla blushed and swatted his shoulder. "Behave."

"Never, woman." Hank lifted her over his shoulder and carried her up the steps and into the house without stumbling once.

When they were gone, Jesse glanced at Corbin. "What do you say, Whitty? Shall we go get our women?"

He was about to say hell, yeah when Mimi

spoke. "Absolutely not. Y'all are in no condition to drive tonight. Tomorrow morning will be soon enough to go get my granddaughters. Now get inside before I switch your bee-hinds."

Once inside, she made them take two aspirins and drink an entire glass of water before she sent them to bed.

As soon as Corbin stepped into his room, Tay greeted him with meows and leg brushes. He scooped her up into his arms and held her close as he made his way to the bed. But before he sat down to take off his boots, he noticed the drawing propped up on the pillows.

He knew his sister's style as soon as he saw it . . . if not the subject. It was another drawing of the Holiday Ranch. But it wasn't one of the drawings she'd done as a teenager. This one was recent. It had all the details right down to the flowers he'd bought to replace the ones Gilley had trampled. Sunny had added a few other details as well: Mimi working in the garden. Hank coming out of the barn. The outline of Darla working in the kitchen. Tay sitting on the porch steps. Gilley racing around the yard.

In the porch swing sat two people.

A man and a woman.

The man was looking at the woman as if she hung the moon. She was looking back at him the same way.

Across the bottom of the drawing were two words.

Cory's Dream.

Chapter Twenty

LIBERTY WAS ON the warpath.

After she and Jesse got in a huge fight, she moved out of Mrs. Fields' and into Cloe's house, then called an emergency Holiday Secret Sisterhood meeting for the following morning.

An in-person meeting.

Noelle came in from Dallas and Hallie from Austin. Since they couldn't go to the Holiday Ranch, the six sisters gathered at the Remington Ranch—sending Rome, Casey, and Sam Remington fleeing as soon as the doorbell started ringing.

Belle hadn't stayed the night with Liberty at the Remington Ranch. Instead, she'd stayed at Corbin's trailer. She had told Liberty it had to do with Sam's No-Animals-in-the-House rule. But secretly she had hoped Corbin would show up.

He hadn't.

Now, there she sat in the midst of her sisters at Cloe's kitchen table, feeling heartbroken. Not because of Corbin's hurtful words. She knew his words and anger had all been a product of his pain. Trust was a huge issue for him. And now the two people he loved the most, Sunny and Jesse, had broken his trust.

He thought Belle had broken it too.

He would never believe she wasn't part of Jesse and Sunny's scheme. There was no way Corbin would believe Liberty had kept it from her. That, and it wasn't like Belle hadn't tricked him before. It made sense she was tricking him again. Still, she wished he had given her the benefit of the doubt. Or at least given her an opportunity to tell her side of things. But she understood why he hadn't. He only knew what he'd been taught—that people you loved couldn't be trusted.

Not that he loved her.

But what if he did?

What if he was just dealing with his pain the same way Liberty was dealing with hers?

"I can't believe I was so gullible!" Liberty brought her fist down on the table, causing all their coffee and tea mugs to jump. "I can't believe I let love cloud my eyes from seeing what a stubborn, opinionated jackass Jesse is. He actually had the gall to defend Corbin after what he did, saying that he was like me and used anger to deal with his pain. I don't use anger to deal with my pain!"

All the sisters glanced at each other as Liberty turned to Belle. "And I just want to say that you were right, Belly. I should never have agreed to marry a man I don't even know. It's a good thing I figured it out before it was too late and broke off the engagement."

A few weeks ago, Belle would have been

thrilled to hear those words. Now, they didn't make her happy. Especially when she could read the heartbreak in her sister's eyes. She completely understood how her sister felt. Her own heart felt like it had been trampled beneath the hoofs of a thousand head of cattle.

She took her sister's hand and squeezed it. "You can't break things off with Jesse, Libby. You love him and I know he loves you."

"Wait a second." Noelle jumped in. "I thought you wanted Liberty and Jesse to break up. Isn't that why you called the last Secret Sisterhood meeting? To figure out how to keep Liberty from marrying Jesse?"

Hallie heaved an exasperated sigh. "Way to spill the beans, Elle."

Liberty jerked her hand from Belle's. "You called a meeting without me? And to break up my engagement?"

Belle nodded. "But now I see what a mistake it was. You love Jesse and you can't let your anger and hurt ruin what you have. Yes, Jesse came up with a bad idea, but he was only trying to do what he thought was right. Which was convince his brother that ranching was harder than he thought and get our family's ranch back. There was only one problem . . . Corbin really does want to be a rancher."

Liberty stared at her. "What are you talking about, Belly? Has sex with Corbin screwed with your head? He doesn't even know how to ride a horse."

Noelle looked at Belle. "You had sex with Corbin? I don't think sleeping with the enemy was what Mimi was talking about when she wanted us to befriend him."

"I wasn't following Mimi's plan," Belle said. "And Corbin is not the enemy."

"He's taking our family's ranch, Belly. What would you call him?"

Belle didn't hesitate to answer. "A man who has never had a place to call home."

"I knew it!" Liberty threw up her hands. "You fell in love with him."

All her sisters turned to her. There was nothing to do but speak the truth.

"Yes. I fell in love with Corbin. If anyone should understand that, Libby, you should. You didn't want to fall in love, but you couldn't stop it. I didn't understand that a few weeks ago. I do now. You can't choose who you fall in love with. It just happens."

"Amen to that," Sweetie said.

"Amen," Cloe echoed.

"Amen," Noelle chimed in. When everyone looked at her with surprise, she shrugged. "I haven't had time to tell y'all that I'm in love with George."

"George?" Sweetie said. "What happened to Luc?"

"Oh. That wasn't love." Noelle's eyes got dreamy. "But what I feel for Georgie is the real thing."

Hallie rolled her eyes. "Y'all have all lost your wits as far as I'm concerned. And I don't care anymore who had sex with who or who y'all think you've fallen in love with. All I care about is the ranch. Are we going to be able to save it or not?"

A sadness filled Belle and it was hard to answer her sister. "The ranch is Corbin's. I think we need to accept that and try to figure out where Daddy, Mama, and Mimi are going to live once they move out at the end of the month."

"Once I get royalty money for my songs," Sweetie said. "Decker and I want to build them a house right next to ours. Until then, they can live with me and Deck."

"You don't have the room, Sweetie," Cloe said. "They can live here."

Hallie shook her head. "Bad idea. I know you think Daddy and Sam have made up, but I think moving them in together is like putting two bulls in the same pen. I'd invite them to come live with me, but Mimi won't be happy living in the city. Besides, there's a good chance I might be jobless soon."

Cloe turned to her. "Why?"

"The brewery I work at was sold and the new owner is an arrogant jerk. Y'all know I struggle to keep my thoughts to myself."

Noelle laughed. "That's putting it mildly, Hal. But if you do get yourself fired, you can come live with me and George in Dallas."

"You're moving in with George? Don't you think that's a little soon?"

"When you know, you know. Georgie has a big old house that will have plenty of room for you and Mama, Daddy, and Mimi. Although you're right. I don't think any of them are going to like living in a big city."

"Then it's a good thing they don't have to."

They all turned to see Sunny standing in the doorway of the kitchen. She lifted a hand in an awkward wave.

"Hey, y'all. I hope you don't mind me comin' on in. I knocked, but you were talking so loudly, you must not have heard." She glanced around. "Please don't tell me this is a Secret Sisterhood meeting? The rumor around high school was that you wore cool matching pink Sisterhood jackets, lit a ton of scented candles, and had a pile of guy voodoo dolls you stuck pins in."

Noelle laughed. "That would have been cool."

Sunny grinned. "It's never too late to change things up. But I didn't come here to talk about pink jackets or voodoo dolls. I came to tell you that Corbin moved out of your family's house. I'm not sure what he plans to do with the ranch. But the house, barn, and acreage they sit on he plans to sign over to your parents and Mimi."

All Belle's sisters jumped up and started hugging each other and Sunny while talking excitedly.

Belle just sat there.

Corbin had left?

She'd thought her heart hurt before. It was nothing compared to how it felt now. While her sisters were celebrating with Sunny, she got up and slipped out of the room. She needed to cry and didn't want to upset her sisters' celebration. Unfortunately, she was stopped before she made it to the front door.

"You love him, don't you?"

Belle turned to find Sunny standing there with a concerned look in her eyes. Belle couldn't have lied if she'd wanted to.

"Yes. But it doesn't matter. He doesn't love me."

"I think you're wrong. Corbin does love you, Belly. But he's not gonna come riding up on a white horse to declare that love. You see, Corbin has never trusted those three words. I think it has to do with my mama saying them every time she dropped us off with another relative. 'I love y'all,' she'd say right before she drove away. Which is why Corbin has no faith in love. But that doesn't mean he doesn't feel it. He just shows his love through actions instead of words."

Images popped into Belle's head. Images of Corbin buying a safety harness for Gilley. Bringing her Flamin' Hot Cheetos and Wild Cherry Pepsi. Worrying about her staying in a seedy hotel or falling out of the hayloft. Thinking of any excuse to stop by the trailer or have her come out to the ranch.

But the sweetest image was of him giving her heated kisses as he ran his hands over her body in soft caresses. It hadn't just been sex. He'd made love to her. Sweet, caring love.

Tears filled Belle's eyes as hope bloomed inside her. "But he thinks I was part of your and Jesse's plan."

"I don't think he thinks that. I think he was just scared of how much he was starting to care for you so he thought he'd push you away before you could push him."

"So what do I do?"

"You do what our mama never could." Sunny smiled, but this time with tears in her eyes. "You don't let him go. Please don't let him go, Belle."

Belle realized Sunny was right. If she was ever going to prove her love to Corbin, she had to do it through actions not words. "Where is he? Did he go back to Houston?"

"Not yet. He's at the trailer. But you need to hurry."

"Tell Cloe to keep an eye on Gilley." Belle turned to head out the door and ran into Jesse. He pulled her into his arms as if he never wanted to let her go before he drew back as if burned.

"Sorry. Wrong Holiday." His eyes were wild and filled with fear. "Please tell me Libby's here, Belle."

"She is."

He sighed with relief. "I guess she's still pissed."

"Yes, and I'm sure she'll explode as soon as you walk into the kitchen."

He smiled. "Then I guess it's a good thing I love fireworks, Belle."

She returned his smile. "I guess it is. And call me Belly."

"Well, don't just stand there grinning, you two," Sunny said. "You got some stubborn hearts to win." She flapped her hands. "Move!"

Belle had never been a fast driver, but she drove like an Indy car racer on the way into town. When she arrived at the trailer, she was relieved to see Corbin's truck parked out front. She didn't knock on the door. Instead, she just walked right in. Corbin sat on the couch eating Flamin' Hot Cheetos and looking like he'd been put through hell. He jumped to his feet when he saw her and her name came out in a croaked voice that broke her heart.

"Bella."

She wanted nothing more than to throw her arms around him and tell him she loved him. But she remembered what Sunny had said and kept those words inside.

At least for now.

She took the bag of Cheetos from him before she sat down on the couch. "So what are we watching?"

"Hope Floats." His voice sounded strained . . . and endearing.

"Good choice." She popped a Cheeto into her mouth and stared at the television, praying he wouldn't ask her to leave. A nerve-wrecking moment later, he joined her on the couch. They continued to pretend to watch the movie until she went to set the bag of Cheetos down on the coffee table and noticed the drawing. A drawing of the ranch with Gilley and Tay and Mama and Daddy and Mimi . . . and her and Corbin.

A drawing that had Cory's Dream written across the bottom.

Tears filled her eyes, but she blinked them back. "Nice drawing."

"It is, isn't it?" He hesitated. "My sister knows me better than I know myself."

She finally turned to him. "Then why did you give the house back?"

"Because that wasn't the most important part of my dream. I didn't realize what the most important part was until I lost it." His eyes held vulnerability . . . but also hope. Hope was a good thing. Hope meant he believed.

She reached out and cradled his face, her thumb tenderly caressing the bruise beneath his eye. "What makes you think you lost it?"

He covered her hand with his and closed his eyes as if her touch healed him. "Did I?"

"How can you ask that question when I'm here, Corbin Whitlock? It's going to take more than a few careless words to get rid of me."

He opened his eyes. "I didn't mean what I said, Bella. It wasn't just sex to me. It was so much more." He hesitated. "I need you."

Because she knew how much he'd been through—how hard he'd worked to prove he didn't need anyone—those words meant more to her than I love you.

"I need you too. I figured that out when I thought you had left and there was this big empty hole in my chest."

He took her hand from his face and placed it over his heart. "This didn't start beating again until you walked through that door. I was going to show up at the Remington Ranch with Jesse . . . but I was scared. Scared you could live without me when I can't live without you."

Tears filled her eyes. Instead of blinking them back, she let them fall.

He pulled her close. "Bella baby, don't cry.

Please don't cry. It breaks my heart when you're sad."

"I'm not sad. I'm happy because you feel the same way I do." She hesitated before she took a leap she hoped wouldn't come back to bite her in the butt. "And since we both can't live without each other, I think we should get married."

His entire body tensed and she rushed on before she lost her nerve.

"I know you're feeling a little blindsided. But you're the one who taught me that when I find something I love, I'll know it. And I love you, Corbin Whitlock. I think I started loving you on our very first date. But I didn't know how much until I got to really know you. And just like lemon drop martinis and Flamin' Hot Cheetos and ornery dogs, now that I've found you, I have no intentions of letting you go. Ever. Because once I love something, I love it for life."

He drew back, his eyes filled with wonder. "You love me?"

"With my whole heart. I know the words don't mean much to you. So I intend to spend the rest of my life showing you just how much. Which is why I think we should get married as soon as possible. I'm thinking the Fourth of July would be nice." She grinned. "Maybe a double wedding with your brother and my ornery sister?"

His eyes widened. "That's only a couple weeks away, Bella."

She frowned. "So when you said you needed me, you meant just for sex."

"No! That's not it at all. I just . . . you want to marry me?"

"Yes, Corbin Whitlock. I want to marry you and spend the rest of my life loving you. Do you have a problem with that?"

He opened his mouth and then closed it. He sat there for a nerve-wrecking moment before a huge smile spread over his face. A smile that lit up the room . . . and her heart.

"Would it matter if I did? If I've learned anything in the last few weeks, it's that once you set your mind to something, Belle Holiday, you can't be dissuaded. So if you want to love me for the rest of our lives, I guess I'll have to let you."

She laughed. "Damn right, you will."

She pushed him back on the couch and started proving her love right then and there.

Chapter Twenty-one

"I THOUGHT I WAS going to gain a brother." Sunny adjusted Corbin's bow tie. "Not lose both of them in one day."

"Aww, I didn't realize how much you love me." Jesse finished pulling on his tuxedo jacket before he reached out to ruffle Sunny's hair.

She swatted his hand away. "Don't mess the hair!" She quickly turned to the mirror to check out the damage. As far as Corbin could tell there wasn't any. She looked stunning in her red bridesmaid's dress with her strawberry-blond hair falling in a cluster of curls down her back.

He stepped behind her and rested his hands on her shoulders. "You look stunning, Sunny. And you're not going to lose Jesse or me. Ever."

"Hell yeah," Jesse said. "You're pretty much stuck with us—and Liberty and Belle."

Sunny turned and her eyes were filled with concern. "Do you think they like me? I mean I know they act like it, but they pretty much have to since they're marrying my brothers."

Usually, Corbin would just tell her she was wrong and go on about his business. But Belle had taught him the importance of valuing other people's feelings. And his own.

"I understand how you feel, Sunny," he said. "There are still times when I feel like an outsider with the Holidays—like I don't belong. But I think those feelings are just the insecurities our parents left us with. They aren't the truth."

Jesse moved up to stand beside him. "Well put, brother." He turned Sunny so all three of them were facing the mirror. "These three good-lookin' siblings do have a lot of baggage from their childhoods, but that doesn't mean they have to carry it around with them for the rest of their lives. Today, let's make a pact to remind each other of that whenever we start to doubt ourselves."

Sunny's eyes lit up. "Maybe we should start our own secret sibling club." She frowned. "Although Whitlock-Cates Secret Sister-Brotherhood just doesn't have a ring to it."

Corbin laughed. "No, it doesn't. Besides, I don't think you'll have time for two secret sibling clubs."

Sunny turned to him. "Two?"

"Way to go, Whitty." Jesse socked him in the arm. "I don't know about Belle, but Liberty is going to give you hell for ruining their surprise."

Corbin cringed as Sunny released a squeal and pulled both him and Jesse in for a jumpy hug.

"I'm going to be a secret sister!" She drew back, her face shining. "They must like me."

"What's not to like?" Jesse went to ruffle her hair again, but stopped when she sent him a warning look. "Okay, no more messing hair.

Now aren't you supposed to be with those secret sisters, fluffing the brides' veils and telling them embarrassing stories about your brothers?"

Her eyes widened. "You're right." She hurried toward the door and then stopped suddenly, turned around, and came back to give Jesse and Corbin each a big kiss on their cheeks. "I love the heck out of you both. And you're right, Cory. I'm not losing brothers. Because y'all will never get away from me." She whirled in a swirl of red material and blond hair before disappearing out the bedroom door.

A smile spread over Jesse's face. "Damn, I love that girl. I understand now why you're so protective of her. She's too sweet to be prepared for the dangers of the world." He looked at Corbin and raised an eyebrow. "So how are we going to get her back here where we can keep an eye on her?"

Corbin smiled slyly as he turned to the mirror and finished adjusting his bow tie. "I'm working on a plan."

Jesse slapped him on the shoulder. "I figured you were. You always have a good plan. Although I'm not so sure your plan of where you're going to live is a good one. I don't know why you and Belle can't just live here at the ranch." He hesitated. "I'm sorry, Whitty. I didn't realize how much you loved this ranch. I just thought it was a whim. I know you gave the house and barn back to the Holidays, but they'd love for you and Belle to live here too."

Mimi, Hank, and Darla had all begged for him and Belle to live with them.

But for some reason, that didn't feel right.

"You once told me this was the Holidays' home—their dream," he said. "And you're right, it is. As much as I've come to love this ranch, I'd also like to have my own home. A home Belle and I build together. Just like you and Liberty are turning Mrs. Fields' Boardinghouse into your dream home."

"I get it," Jesse said. "But I hope you'll still run the ranch. I hate to say it, but I don't think Hank can handle it alone."

"Neither can I, and I've discovered I don't want the entire responsibility of the ranch on my shoulders. I still want to run my investment company and I want plenty of time to spend with Belle. Which is why I'm hiring a foreman."

"Do you have a clue who you'll hire?"

"No. I've interviewed a lot of cowboys, but Hank vetoed all of them. He's a hard man to please. We're lucky he didn't veto us."

"You're right." Jesse slipped an arm around Corbin shoulders. "Now let's go marry our women before he changes his mind."

"I will never complain about another stressed-out bride again." Liberty stared at her reflection in the mirror. "And whose idea was it to let Sissy Haskins fix our hair?"

Belle bit back a smile as she adjusted the veil on her sister's massive up-do. "Yours."

"Damn. You should have talked me out of it. Along with this tight corset dress." Liberty tugged on the bodice of her wedding gown. "I can't breathe in this contraption."

"You can't breathe because you're nervous. All brides are."

Liberty looked at her in the mirror. "You're not."

It was true. Belle wasn't nervous. She was excited and happier than she'd felt in a long time. After years of letting her sister make all the decisions, Belle had finally discovered what she wanted.

And who she was.

She was the calm, collected twin. The sister who put people at ease and kept her head in stressful situations. The sister who wasn't loud and assertive, but still knew how to get her way. The sister who loved watching people celebrate the most important moments of their lives.

Today, she finally got to celebrate her own important moment. She was marrying exactly the type of man she had always dreamed about. A man who was kind and protective ... and vulnerable. A man who was scared of love, but when he loved, loved deeply.

Corbin loved her deeply.

She didn't doubt it for a second.

As soon as Belle had finished adjusting Liberty's veil, the rest of the bridal party started showing up. As the maids of honor, Sweetie and Cloe wore navy blue dresses. The bridesmaids, Hallie, Noelle, and Sunny, wore red. And the flower girl, Pip Wadley, wore a mixture of red, white, and blue.

She looked absolutely adorable.

As did Buck and Gilley with their stars and stripes collars. The wedding bands were attached to those collars, which made Belle a little nervous. She hoped Gilley wouldn't break away from Pip as they walked down the aisle. Although the little girl seemed to have a way with animals just like her grandma Melba. The entire time the bridal party was adjusting bows and doing last-minute primping, Pip was teaching both dogs how to sit and stay by using the dog treats she had stashed in her dress pocket.

"That little gal is a chip off the old block." Mimi moved up next to Belle. She wore a red, white, and blue flowered dress with a wide-brimmed hat decorated with matching flowers. She looked as happy as Belle . . . until her gaze landed on Hallie, who was standing at the window waiting for Daddy's signal that it was time for the bridal party to head over. "I'm worried about Halloween," Mimi said.

Hallie had been fired from her job at a brewery in Austin. Belle had been so busy with Corbin and planning the wedding, she hadn't had much chance to talk to her little sister. That, and Hallie had always been so strong, Belle never worried about her.

She turned to her grandmother. "I don't think you need to worry, Mimi. She told me she wasn't that upset about being fired. The new owner of the brewery was a real jerk she's happy to be away from. And I'm sure she won't have any problems finding another job."

"I'm not worried about her finding another job. I'm worried about her moving back to a big city where she has no one to watch out for her. I understand all young people wanting to move away from home and sow their wild oats, but she's done that and I think her getting fired is a sign from God that it's time for her to move back home and be surrounded by people who love her."

Belle smiled. "You want all your granddaughters to move back home."

"And what's wrong with that? Look how happy you, Liberty, Sweetie, and Cloe are now that you've moved back. Now all we need to do is convince Hallie and Noelle to do the same and the family will be all together again."

Before she could tell her grandmother it wasn't likely Hallie and Noelle would move back home, Hallie spoke in a high-pitched squeak that drew everyone's attention. Hallie had never spoken in squeaks in her life. She usually spoke in bellows.

"Jace?"

Noelle joined Hallie at the window. "Lord have mercy. It is Jace Carson. I thought he was living in Galveston with his mama after leaving that Canadian football team. All I can say is no wonder he had a fan club that called themselves Jace's Junkies. The man is sex in a Stetson."

"I remember hearing about Jace Carson." Sunny joined Noelle and Hallie at the window. Belle had to admit the three women looked stunning together. Sunny with her long strawberry-blond hair, Hallie with even longer wheat-colored hair, and Noelle with her short black hair. "Is he the guy talking to your daddy?" Sunny asked. "He is hot."

Noelle sighed. "Too bad he's covered by the Secret Sister oath."

Hallie started choking and Belle hurried over to thump her on the back. "Are you okay, Hal?"

Hallie cleared her throat. "Fine. Just fine."

But she didn't look fine. She looked as white as Belle's dress. Belle had to wonder if maybe Mimi was right. Maybe Hallie did need a break from big city life. Or maybe she was just worried that most of her sisters were starting families of their own and would forget about her. Belle decided right then and there to spend more time with her sister.

"The Secret Sister oath?" Sunny asked. "What's that?"

"It's an oath we all took when we were younger," Noelle explained. "No dating, or hooking up with, other sisters' boyfriends—past or present." She sent Sunny a pointed look. "Everyone who joins our club has to take the oath."

Sunny nodded sagely. "I would never poach on any of y'all's boyfriends." She hesitated. "None of you have dated Casey Remington, right?"

Noelle visibly blanched before she pinned on a smile. "Absolutely not. Casey Remington is nothing to me. Absolutely nothing. Kenny is the love of my life."

"Kenny?" Belle asked. "What happened to George?"

"He was much too clingy. But Kenny is the perfect—"

Belle cut her off when she glanced out the window and saw Daddy waving. "We'll have to hear about your perfect man later, Elle. It's time."

Liberty turned from the mirror. "It's time?" She looked terrified. Belle figured it was up to her to make sure her sister didn't bolt.

"Pip, get the dogs on their leashes and everyone head to the barn and line up in the order we practiced last night. Libby and I will be there shortly."

Once everyone was gone, Belle walked over to her sister and took her hands. "It's okay, Libby. This is the day we dreamed about. We always knew we'd walk down the aisle together on Daddy's arms and that's exactly what we're going to do." She smiled. "We even planned on marrying brothers."

The fear left Liberty's eyes, and she smiled. "First dibs on Nick Jonas."

Belle laughed. "I think the Cates/Whitlock brothers are much better looking than any ol' Jonas. Now let's go get our brothers."

Overwhelming joy filled Belle when she saw Corbin waiting for her in the barn. He looked so handsome in his tuxedo it took her breath away. Or maybe it was the look in his cobalt-blue eyes that took her breath away. There was no vulnerability or fear.

Just pure love.

When he spoke his vows, his voice was strong and steady. She knew in her heart that his love would be the same. After the preacher had pronounced them husband and wife, Corbin lifted her veil and kissed her. Or she kissed him. It didn't matter. All that mattered was that she would remember the kiss for the rest of her life.

After following Jesse and Liberty down the aisle, she and Corbin were supposed to pose for photographs. But as soon as they got outside, Corbin drew her around to the paddock where Homer and Sadie Mae were saddled and waiting. Most brides would have asked what was going on, but Belle didn't. She knew Corbin wasn't a man who did things randomly. He had planned this . . . for her. So she didn't say a word. She just gathered the train of her dress, thanked the Lord she was wearing boots, and allowed Corbin to help her mount.

She smiled when they headed straight for Cooper Springs. The smile faded when he led her around the trees to a plot of land that had been corded off with string and wooden stakes.

"What's this?"

He glanced over at her. Once again, he looked uncertain and vulnerable. "A front porch. Or at least, it will be one once we start building. I didn't want to come up with any plans for the rest of the house without your input, but I thought it was safe to plan the front porch. A big front porch with plenty of room for a porch swing and decorations for every holiday." He paused. "And a rocker to rock our babies."

She couldn't help it. Tears started falling. Corbin quickly dismounted and helped her down. Once she was in his arms, he cradled her face and brushed the tears from her cheeks.

"I hope these are happy tears, Bella."

"The happiest. So I guess you read my letter." The guilty flush was answer enough. She laughed. "So you also know I really wanted Nick Jonas."

"Yes. But I'm afraid you'll have to live without him."

She heaved an exaggerated sigh. "And I was so counting on my husband singing to me every morning and night."

"I'm afraid I can't sing, but I can do something else every morning and night."

"And what's that?"

His eyes were intense and sincere. "Tell you I love you."

That was even better.

Epilogue

"JUST WHERE ARE you taking me, Jesse Cates?" Liberty struggled to keep her wedding dress from dragging on the ground as Jesse led her across the pasture behind the barn.

The wedding reception was winding down and most people had already headed home. Which was exactly where Liberty wanted to go. She and Jesse had partied with the townsfolk and danced the night away. Now, she was ready to head home to the bed-and-breakfast where she intended to make love to her new husband until dawn.

But Jesse seemed to have other ideas.

"Where do you think I'm going, darlin'? I'm taking you to my absolute favorite place in the whole wide world—the place where I first met a wildcat that changed my life forever."

She smiled as she stumbled behind him. "Cooper Springs."

He glanced over his shoulder at her and his teeth flashed in the darkness. "That would be the place. You ready to get your butt whooped, Libby Lou?"

"That depends. Are we talking about swimming or sex?"

With a shouted laugh he whirled and picked her up, swinging her around until she was giggling. "God, I love you."

She loved him too. She thanked God every day that he hadn't let her temper keep them from getting married. There was only one man she wanted to spend the rest of her life with . . . even if he had more energy than she did.

"It's one o'clock in the morning, Jess," she said when he set her back on her feet. "Couldn't we wait and go to Cooper Springs tomorrow?"

"Now, darlin', are you saying you're too tired to beat me in a challenge?"

She scowled. "Never."

He winked. "That's my feisty gal."

When they arrived at Cooper Springs, Liberty was surprised to find multiple camp lanterns encircling two sleeping bags spread out close to the water. An open cooler with bottles of champagne sat on a nearby rock.

She smiled. "So sex was on the agenda."

"You know making love to you is always on my agenda." He pulled her into his arms and kissed her. A sweet, loving kiss that made her melt. But before she could deepen it, a rustling sound had her drawing back.

Mickey Gilley burst through the trees, followed by Buck Owens. The huge dog hit Liberty at full gallop and would have knocked her to the ground if Jesse hadn't been holding her. She laughed as the dog covered her face with sloppy kisses while

Buck wedged his fat body in between her and Gilley, begging for his own attention.

Jesse sighed heavily. "Well, I guess both sex and swimming are out of the question now. Buck almost drowned last time he followed us into the springs. I guess we'll have to settle for cuddling and looking at . . . the stars."

"That sounds perfect to me." She gave Gilley and Buck good ear scratches before returning her attention to Jesse. "I'll whoop your butt later—at swimming and sex."

"I look forward to it, darlin'." He kissed her. But once again, it was cut short by a rustling. This time Belle and Corbin stepped out of the trees. Belle had the train of her wedding dress hooked over one arm and Tay cradled in the other. She looked as surprised to see Liberty, as Liberty was to see her.

"Libby?"

"Belly?"

They greeted each other with a tight hug before they turned to their new husbands and spoke at the same time. "What's going on?"

Jesse and Corbin exchanged grins before Jesse spoke. "We planned a little surprise for y'all. Shall we get comfy?" He toed off his boots and started to take off his tuxedo jacket when Liberty stopped him.

"Now hold on right there, Jesse Cates. Belle and I might have occasionally pulled the twin switch, but if you think we're going to do the twin swap, you got another think coming."

Both Jesse's and Corbin's eyes widened before they busted out laughing. Corbin sobered first.

"I'm not into twin switching or swapping." He pulled Belle close and looked at her as if she hung the moon. "You're the only twin for me, Bella."

Belle smiled at her husband. "Then what's the surprise?"

"You'll see." Jesse said. "For now, let's pop open that champagne."

When everyone had a Solo cup of champagne, Corbin held his up and made a toast. "To the twin sisters who gave these two ornery brothers something they always wanted . . . the love of a good woman and a place to call home."

"Amen to that," Jesse said. "Corbin and I both thank our lucky stars every day that we found our Fourth of July girls."

Before Liberty could blink back the tears that had formed in her eyes, Jesse whistled loudly. A second later, there was a series of sizzling pops and trailing lights shot up into the sky before exploding into blooms of brilliant fireworks.

Liberty had no more gotten over the breathtaking sight then the rest of her family and Jesse's family burst through the trees, yelling "Happy Birthday!" Mama carried a small cake with lit candles that Shirlene, Jesse's mama, held her cupped hands around so they wouldn't blow out in the summer breeze. All her and Jesse's sisters carried paper plates, napkins, and presents, while the rest of the Cateses and Holidays trailed behind talking and laughing.

There was no blinking back the tears this time.

When she glanced over at Belle, her sister was crying too. They smiled at each other, communicating their feelings without one word.

They were blessed.

Truly blessed.

"What do you think, Libby Lou?" Jesse asked. "Is this enough fireworks for you?"

Liberty turned to her new husband. He was smiling that smile that made her heart burst as brightly as the shimmering display exploding overhead.

She hooked her arms around his neck. "Nope. But I figure we have the rest of our lives to make fireworks."

THE END

Turn the page for a Sneak Peek of the next Holiday Ranch!

Sneak Peek!
Wrangling a Texas Hometown Hero

Chapter One

Whoever said you couldn't drown your sorrows in alcohol was wrong.

After three beers and an equal amount of tequila shots, Jace Carson was feeling no pain. In fact, he was feeling quite content. He figured more alcohol would make him feel even better. A few minutes later, Jace had another beer and a shot of tequila in front of him. He toasted the bartender who had brought them.

"To good women, good times, and good bartenders." He downed the tequila before chasing it with a swig of beer.

The bartender, who looked too young to be serving liquor, smiled. "So what's your story, man?"

"My story?"

"Yeah. There are all different types that walk through those doors. Some come in because they're lonely and looking to hook up or just share a drink with other lonely people. Some come in to watch sporting events without screaming kids or nagging wives. And some people come in to get drunk and forget about their problems. Since you haven't hit on that hot woman at the end of the bar or glanced once at the baseball game on the television, I'm going to say you're here to forget."

Jace lifted his beer in a silent salute. "Smart man." As he took a drink, he couldn't help glancing down the bar at the woman. It showed how preoccupied he'd been with drowning his sorrows that he hadn't noticed her.

She wore a flat-brimmed western hat—the kind country singer Lainey Wilson wore. The hat, combined with the dark bar, kept Jace from seeing her face, but he could see the wealth of wheat-colored that hung in golden waves well past the edge of the bar.

He'd always been a sucker for long, blond hair.

He lowered his glass and smiled at the bartender. "Although hot women work just as well at making you forget your troubles." He started to get up, but the bartender stopped him.

"You might want to think twice about trying for that one. She's already turned down two guys ... and harshly. When I brought her the beer she ordered, she took one sip and informed me it was the worst shit she'd ever tasted. After that, she's been ordering tequila shots. I think she's got some troubles of her own."

Jace smiled. "Then we're a match made in heaven." He grabbed his beer and got to his feet. The room wobbled. He took a moment to steady himself before he carefully made his way to the other end of the bar.

The woman didn't even glance over when he took a seat next to her.

This close, he could see the profile of the lower half of her face that wasn't shadowed by the hat. Hot wasn't the word he'd use. She was more cute. She had a button nose with freckles sprinkling the bridge, a heart-shaped face, and a mouth with pouty lips that begged for a good kissing.

Okay, maybe she was hot.

She was petite with full breasts that filled out a T-shirt with a beer logo on the front. The blue-jeaned butt seated on the barstool would fit real nice in his hands. Cowboy boots finished off her outfit. Not the designer kind most girls wore to a bar. These boots were scuffed and well worn. He could easily picture them hooked in the stirrups of a saddle . . . or wrapped around his waist.

But before he could start flirting his way into her bed, she spoke.

"I'm not interested, cowboy. So please don't waste your time coming up with some ridiculous pick-up line. Believe me, I've heard them all."

"All of them?" Jace squinted at the firm set of her jaw. "Really? So you've heard—'You know what you'd look beautiful in? My arms.' or 'I love my bed, but I'd rather be in yours.' Or what about 'This might sound cheesy, but I think you're grate.'—Get it? G-r-a-t-e. Grate. Or my favorite, 'I'd give up my morning cereal to spoon with you instead.'"

A husky laugh burst out of those pouty lips. The kind of laugh that made a man think of cool bed sheets and hot naked skin. "I'm still not interested," she said. "But the last one wasn't half bad."

Her comment gave Jace the motivation to keep flirting, but his next words got stuck in his throat when she turned to him. He was drunk, but not drunk enough to ignore the ping of recognition that went off in his brain.

He'd met this woman before.

He stared at her and tried to blink away the blurring at the edge of his vision. "Do I know you?"

She laughed that husky laugh. "Now that is the worst pick-up line."

"No. I'm serious. I think we've met before."

She sobered and reached out to tip up his cowboy hat. Her lips parted on a startled inhalation of breath. "Jace . . . Jace Carson."

He tried to figure out how he knew her. Seeing as how he was already physically attracted to her, he figured they'd hooked up before. If he couldn't remember her name, that wouldn't be good.

"Uhh . . . hey."

A smirk lifted the corners of her kissable mouth. "You don't recognize me, do you?" She placed a hand on her chest. "I'm heartbroken. And here I thought you and I had a lifelong connection since I pretty much have known you since I was in diapers." She tipped up her own hat to reveal eyes the exact shade of a lush spring meadow. Jace felt like a three-hundred-pound tackle had sacked him. He knew the color of these eyes. They had haunted his dreams since he was fourteen years old.

Sweetie Holiday had been his high school sweetheart and the only woman he'd ever loved. When she had broken up with him their senior year, he'd been devastated. But he'd dealt with the pain and gotten over her ... until she'd gone and fallen in love with his cousin. Then all those feelings of not being good enough had resurfaced and he was still struggling to come to terms with the fact that Decker was able to hold onto Sweetie when Jace couldn't.

That seemed to be the theme of Jace's life. He struggled to hold onto anything he loved deeply.

Sweetie.

Football.

His father.

"You still with me, Jace?"

He blinked out of his daze and stared at the woman sitting next to him. Same color of eyes. But different girl. Sweetie's little sister.

"Well, I'll be damned. How are you, Teeny Weeny?"

The smile turned into a frown. "That has to be the worst nickname ever."

"Would you rather I call you by your real name ... Halloween Holiday?"

"Not unless you want your balls relocated into your ears. I prefer Hallie and, after knowing me for most of my life, you damn well know it."

"I do, but that doesn't mean I'm going to stop calling you Teeny Weeny—not when you won the hot dog eating contest when you were only ten years old. I still can't believe you put away eleven hot dogs without throwing up."

"Oh, I threw up. But only after I got my ribbon."

He laughed again. It felt good. He couldn't remember the last time he'd laughed without forcing it. He sobered and looked at her. Hallie had definitely outgrown the nickname. She was no longer the feisty little tomboy who used to follow him all over the Holiday Ranch giving him pointers on how to win the next high school football game. She was a beautiful woman.

Although she was still feisty.

"Damn, you look like hell," she said. "Is that scruffy thing on your face supposed to be a beard?"

He ran a hand over his whiskered jaw. "I misplaced my razor and just haven't bought a new one." It was a lie. The truth was he just didn't care about shaving . . . or anything, really.

"You know they sell razors online and ship them right to your house. It's the wonder of online shopping. And speaking of houses, don't tell me you live here in Austin now."

He knew whatever he shared with Hallie would be shared with Sweetie and her four other sisters—who would then share it with the rest of the Holidays and subsequently the entire town of Wilder, Texas. While everyone at home probably already knew about his career-ending injury, he didn't want them knowing about his pathetic attempt to keep playing football.

"No. I don't live here. I'm just passing through. What are you doing here?"

"I live just a few blocks away."

"And you always stop by for shitty beer and tequila?"

A defeated look settled over her face. He understood the look well. "It's been one helluva day."

He nodded. "Yeah. I get it. Although it's been more of a helluva year for me."

A mischievous twinkle entered her green eyes. "Then maybe I should buy you a drink."

Order
WRANGLING A TEXAS HOMETOWN HERO Now!

https://katielanebooks.com/wrangling-a-texas-hometown-hero

Also by Katie Lane

Be sure to check out all of Katie Lane's novels!
www.katielanebooks.com

HOLIDAY RANCH SERIES
Wrangling a Texas Sweetheart
Wrangling a Lucky Cowboy
Wrangling a Texas Firecracker
Wrangling a Hot Summer Cowboy
Wrangling a Texas Hometown Hero—coming August 30

KINGMAN RANCH SERIES
Charming a Texas Beast
Charming a Knight in Cowboy Boots
Charming a Big Bad Texan
Charming a Fairytale Cowboy
Charming a Texas Prince
Charming a Christmas Texan
Charming a Cowboy King

BAD BOY RANCH SERIES
Taming a Texas Bad Boy
Taming a Texas Rebel
Taming a Texas Charmer
Taming a Texas Heartbreaker
Taming a Texas Devil

Taming a Texas Rascal
Taming a Texas Tease
Taming a Texas Christmas Cowboy

BRIDES OF BLISS TEXAS SERIES
Spring Texas Bride
Summer Texas Bride
Autumn Texas Bride
Christmas Texas Bride

TENDER HEART TEXAS SERIES
Falling for Tender Heart
Falling Head Over Boots
Falling for a Texas Hellion
Falling for a Cowboy's Smile
Falling for a Christmas Cowboy

DEEP IN THE HEART OF TEXAS SERIES
Going Cowboy Crazy
Make Mine a Bad Boy
Catch Me a Cowboy
Trouble in Texas
Flirting with Texas
A Match Made in Texas
The Last Cowboy in Texas
My Big Fat Texas Wedding

OVERNIGHT BILLIONAIRES SERIES
A Billionaire Between the Sheets
A Billionaire After Dark
Waking up with a Billionaire

HUNK FOR THE HOLIDAYS SERIES
Hunk for the Holidays
Ring in the Holidays
Unwrapped

About the Author

KATIE LANE IS a firm believer that love conquers all and laughter is the best medicine. Which is why you'll find plenty of humor and happily-ever-afters in her contemporary and western contemporary romance novels. A USA Today Bestselling Author, she has written numerous series, including Deep in the Heart of Texas, Hunk for the Holidays, Overnight Billionaires, Tender Heart Texas, The Brides of Bliss Texas, Bad Boy Ranch, Kingman Ranch, and Holiday Ranch. Katie lives in Albuquerque, New Mexico, and when she's not writing, she enjoys reading, eating chocolate (dark, please), and snuggling with her high school sweetheart and cairn terrier, Roo.

For more on her writing life or just to chat, check out Katie here:
FACEBOOK
www.facebook.com/katielaneauthor
INSTAGRAM
www.instagram.com/katielanebooks.

And for more information on upcoming releases and great giveaways, be sure to sign up for her mailing list at www.katielanebooks.com!

Printed in Great Britain
by Amazon